what are you going through

what
are
you
going
through

sigrid
nunez

virago

VIRAGO

First published in the United States in 2020 by Riverhead Books
First published in Great Britain in 2020 by Virago Press

1 3 5 7 9 10 8 6 4 2

A CIP catalogue record for this book
is available from the British Library.

Hardback ISBN 978-0-349-01366-4
Trade paperback ISBN 978-0-349-01367-1

Book design by Lucia Bernard

Printed and bound in Great Britain by Clays Ltd, Elcograf S.p.A.

Papers used by Virago are from well-managed forests
and other responsible sources.

Virago Press
An imprint of
Little, Brown Book Group
Carmelite House
50 Victoria Embankment
London EC4Y 0DZ

An Hachette UK Company
www.hachette.co.uk

www.virago.co.uk.

what are you going through

PART ONE

The love of our neighbor in all its fullness
simply means being able to say to him,
"What are you going through?"

—*Simone Weil*

I went to hear a man give a talk. The event was held on a college campus. The man was a professor, but he taught at a different school, in another part of the country. He was a well-known author, who, earlier that year, had won an international prize. But although the event was free and open to the public, the auditorium was only half full. I myself would not have been in the audience, I would not even have been in that town, had it not been for a coincidence. A friend of mine was being treated in a local hospital that specializes in treating her particular type of cancer. I had come to visit this friend, this very dear old friend whom I had not seen in several years, and whom, given the gravity of her illness, I might not see again.

It was the third week of September, 2017. I had booked

a room through Airbnb. The host was a retired librarian, a widow. From her profile I knew that she was also the mother of four, the grandmother of six, and that her hobbies included cooking and going to the theater. She lived on the top floor of a small condo about two miles from the hospital. The apartment was clean and tidy and smelled faintly of cumin. The guest room was decorated in the way that most people appear to have agreed will make a person feel at home: plush area rugs, a bed with a hedge of pillows and a plump down duvet, a small table holding a ceramic pitcher of dried flowers, and, on the nightstand, a stack of paperback mysteries. The kind of place where I never do feel at home. What most people call cozy—gemütlich, hygge—others find stifling.

A cat had been promised, but I saw no sign of one. Only later, when it was time for me to leave, would I learn that, between my booking and my stay, the host's cat had died. She delivered this news brusquely, immediately changing the subject so that I couldn't ask her about it—which I was in fact going to do only because something in her manner made me think that she wanted to be asked about it. And it occurred to me that maybe it wasn't emotion that had made her change the subject like that but rather worry that I might later complain. *Depressing host talked too much about dead cat.* The sort of comment you saw on the site all the time.

In the kitchen, as I drank the coffee and ate from the tray of snacks the host had prepared for me (while she, in the way recommended for Airbnb hosts, made herself scarce), I studied the corkboard where she posted publicity for guests about goings-on in town. An exhibition of Japanese prints, an arts-and-crafts fair, a visiting Canadian dance company, a jazz festival, a Caribbean culture festival, a schedule for the local sports arena, a spoken-word reading. And, that night, at seven thirty, the author's talk.

In the photograph, he looks harsh—no, "harsh" is too harsh. Call it stern. That look that comes to many older white men at a certain age: stark-white hair, beaky nose, thin lips, piercing gaze. Like raptors. Hardly inviting. Hardly an image to say, *Please, do come hear me speak. Would love to see you there!* More like, *Make no mistake, I know a lot more than you do. You should listen to me. Maybe then you'll know what's what.*

A woman introduces him. The head of the department that has invited him to speak. She is a familiar type: the glam academic, the intellectual vamp. Someone at pains for it to be known that, although smart and well educated, although a feminist and a woman in a position of power, the lady is no frump, no boring nerd, no sexless harridan. And so what if she's past a certain age. The cling of the skirt, the height of the heels, the scarlet mouth and tinted hair (I once heard a salon colorist say, I believe it's got to hurt a woman's ability to think if she has gray hair), everything says: I'm still fuck-able. A slimness that almost certainly means going much of each day feeling hungry. It crosses such women's minds with some sad regularity that *in France* intellectuals can be sex symbols. Even if the symbol can sometimes be embarrassing (Bernard-Henri Lévy and his unbuttoned shirts). These women have memories of being tormented in girlhood, not for their looks but for their brains. "Men don't make passes at girls who wear glasses" really meant smart girls, bookish girls, mathletes, and science geeks. Times change. Now who doesn't love eyewear. Now how common is it to hear a man boast about his attraction to smart women. Or, as one young actor recently shared: I've always felt that the sexiest women are the ones with the biggest brains. At which I confess I rolled my eyes so hard that I had to toss my head to get them to come down again.

It cannot possibly be true, can it, the story about Toscanini losing patience during a rehearsal with a soprano, grabbing her large breasts and crying, If only these were brains!

Later came "Men don't make passes at girls with fat asses."

I can see them, this man and this woman, at the department dinner that will surely follow the event, and which, because of who he is, will be a fine one, at one of the area's most expensive restaurants, and where it's likely they'll be seated next to each other. And of course the woman will be hoping for some intense conversation—no small talk—maybe even a bit of flirtation, but this will turn out to be not so easy given how his attention keeps straying to the far end of the table, to the grad student who's been assigned as his escort, responsible for shuttling him from place to place, including after tonight's dinner back to his hotel, and who, after just one glass of wine, is responding to his frequent glances with increasingly bold ones of her own.

It looks like it might be true. I googled it. According to some reports, though, he didn't actually grab the soprano's breasts but only pointed at them.

During the obligatory recitation of the speaker's accomplishments, the man lowers his gaze and assumes a grimace of discomfort in an affectation of modesty that I doubt fools anyone.

If grades had depended more on how much I absorbed from lectures than from studying texts, I'd have failed out of school. I don't often lose concentration when I'm reading something or listening to a person converse, but talks of any kind have always given me trouble (the worst being authors reading from their own work). My mind starts wandering almost as soon as the speaker gets started. Also, this particular evening I was unusually distracted. I had spent all afternoon in the hospital with my friend. I was wrung out from watching her suffer, and from trying not to let my dismay at her condition get the better of me and become obvious to her. Dealing with illness: I've never been good at that, either.

So my mind wandered. It wandered right from the start. I lost the thread of the talk several times. But it hardly mattered, because the man's talk was based on a long article he had written for a magazine, and I had read the article when it came out. I had read it, and everyone I knew had read it.

My friend in the hospital had read it. My guess was, most people in the audience had too. It occurred to me that at least some of them had come because they wanted to ask questions, to hear a discussion of what the man had to say, the substance of which they were already familiar with from the article. But the man had made the unusual decision not to take any questions. There was to be no discussion tonight. This, however, we wouldn't know until after he'd finished speaking.

It was all over, he said. He quoted another writer, translating from the French: Before man, the forest; after him, the desert. Whatever must be done to forestall catastrophe, whatever actions or sacrifices, it was now clear that humankind lacked the will, the collective will, to undertake them. To any intelligent alien, he said, we would appear to be in the grip of a death wish.

It was over, he said again. No more the faith and consolation that had sustained generations and generations, the knowledge that, though our own individual time on earth must end, what we loved and what had meaning for us would go on, the world of which we had been a part would endure—that time had ended, he said. Our world and our civilization would not endure, he said. We must live and die in this new knowledge.

Our world and our civilization would not endure, the man said, because they could not survive the many forces we ourselves had set against it. We, our own worst enemy, had set ourselves up like sitting ducks, allowing weapons capable of killing us all many times over not only to be created but also to land in the hands of egomaniacs, nihilists, men without empathy, without conscience. Between our failure to control the spread of WMDs and our failure to keep from power those for whom their use was not only thinkable but perhaps even an irresistible temptation, apocalyptic war was becoming increasingly likely. . . .

When we go, the man said, pretty as it might be to think so, we will not be replaced by a race of noble and intelligent apes. Comforting, perhaps, to imagine that, with humans extinct, the planet might have a chance. Alas, the animal kingdom was doomed, he said. Though none of the evil would be of their making, the apes and all the other creatures were doomed along with us—those that human activity would not have annihilated already, that is.

But say there was no nuclear threat, the man said. Say, by some miracle, the world's entire nuclear arsenal had been pulverized overnight. Would we not still be faced with the perils that generations of human stupidity, shortsightedness, and capacity for self-delusion had produced. . . .

The fossil fuel industrialists, the man said. How many were they, how many were *we*? It beggared belief that we, a free people, citizens of a democracy, had failed to stop them, had failed to stand up to these men and their political enablers working so assiduously at climate change denial. And to think that these same people had already reaped profits of billions, making them some of the richest people ever to have lived. But when the most powerful nation in the world took their side, swaggered to the very forefront of denial, what hope did Planet Earth have. To think that the masses of refugees fleeing shortages of food and clean water caused by global ecological disaster would find compassion anywhere their desperation drove them was absurd, the man said. On the contrary, we would soon see man's inhumanity to man on a scale like nothing that had ever been seen before.

The man was a good speaker. He had an iPad on the lectern in front of him, to which his gaze fell from time to time, but instead of reading straight from the text he spoke as though he'd memorized every line. In that way he was like an actor. A good actor. He was very good. Not once did he hesitate or stumble over a word, but nor did the talk come off as rehearsed. A gift. He spoke with authority and was nothing if not convincing, clearly sure of everything he said. As in the article I'd read and on which the talk was based, he supported his statements with numerous references. But there was also something about him that said that he didn't really care about being convincing. It was not a matter of opinion, what he said, it was irrefutable fact. It made no difference whether you believed him or not. This being the case, it struck me as odd, it struck me as really truly odd, his giving that talk. I had thought, because he was addressing people in the flesh, people who'd come out to hear him, that he would take a different tone from the one I remembered from the magazine article. I had thought that this time there'd be some, if not sanguine, at least not utterly doomster takeaway; a gesture, at least, to some possible way forward; a crumb, if only a crumb it be, of hope. As in, Now that I've got your attention, now that I've scared the bejesus out of you, let's talk about what might be done. Otherwise, why talk to us at all, sir? This, I was sure, was what other people in the audience must also have been feeling.

Cyberterrorism. Bioterrorism. The inevitable next great flu pandemic, for which we were, just as inevitably, unprepared. Incurable killer infections borne of our indiscriminate use of antibiotics. The rise of far-right regimes around the world. The normalization of propaganda and deceit as political strategy and basis for government policy. The inability to defeat global jihadism. Threats to life and liberty—to anything worthy of the name civilization—were flourishing, the man said. In short supply, on the other hand, were the means to combat them. . . .

And who could believe that the concentration of such vast power in the hands of a few tech corporations—not to mention the system for mass surveillance on which their dominance and profits depended—could be in humanity's future best interests. Who could seriously doubt that these companies' tools might one day become the most amazingly effective means to the most ruthless imaginable ends. Yet how helpless we were before our tech gods and masters, the man said. It was a good question, he said: Just how many more opioids could Silicon Valley come up with before it was all over. What would life be like when the system ensured that the individual no longer even had the option to say no to being followed everywhere and constantly shouted at and poked like an animal in a cage. Again, how had a supposedly freedom-loving people allowed this to happen? Why were people not outraged by the very idea of surveillance capitalism? Scared right out of their wits by Big Tech? An alien one day studying our collapse might well conclude: Freedom was too much for them. They would rather be slaves.

A person who only read the man's words, rather than hearing and watching him speak, would probably have imagined him quite different from the way he actually was that night. Given the words, the meaning, the horrific *facts*, a person would probably imagine some show of emotion. Not these calm, cadenced sentences. Not this dispassionate mask. Only once did I catch a flicker of feeling: when he was talking about the animals, a slight catch in his throat. For humans, there seemed to be no pity in him. From time to time as he spoke, he looked out over the lectern and raked the audience with his raptor's gaze. Later, I thought I understood why he hadn't wanted to take questions. Have you ever been at a Q&A where at least one person did not make some thoughtless remark or ask the kind of irrelevant question that suggested that they hadn't been listening to a thing the speaker just said? I could see how, for this speaker, after this talk, something like that would have been unendurable.

Maybe he was afraid he'd lose his temper. Because of course it was there: Beneath the cool, the control, you could sense it. Deep and volcanic emotion. Which, were he to allow himself to express it, would spew out of the top of his head and burn us all to ash.

There was something strange, too, even bizarre, I thought, about the behavior of the audience. So meek before that grim portrait of their future, the even grimmer one said to be in store for their kids. Such calm and polite attention, as if the speaker had not been describing a time when, in a ghastly reversal of the natural order, first the young would envy the old—a stage already in progress, according to him—then the living would envy the dead.

What a thing to put your hands together for, but that is what we did, as I suppose it would have been even stranger for us not to have done—but now I'm getting ahead of myself.

Before the applause, before the end of the talk, the man brought up something that did in fact cause a ripple on that smooth surface. A murmur passed through the audience (which the man ignored), people shifted in their seats, and I noticed a few headshakes, and, from a row somewhere behind me, a woman's nervous laugh.

It was over, he said. It was too late, we had dithered too long. Our society had already become too fragmented and dysfunctional for us to fix, in time, the calamitous mistakes we had made. And, in any case, people's attention remained elusive. Neither season after season of extreme weather events nor the risk of extinction for a million animal species around the world could push environmental destruction to the top of our country's list of concerns. And how sad, he said, to see so many among the most creative and best-educated classes, those from whom we might have hoped for inventive solutions, instead embracing personal therapies and pseudo-religious practices that promoted detachment, a focus on the moment, acceptance of one's surroundings as they were, equanimity in the face of worldly cares. (*This world is but a shadow, it is a carcass, it is nothing, this world is not real, do not mistake this hallucination for the real world.*) Self-care, relieving one's own everyday anxieties, avoiding stress: these had become some of our society's highest goals, he said—higher, apparently, than the salvation of society itself. The mindfulness rage was just another distraction, he said. *Of course* we should be stressed, he said. We should be utterly *consumed* with dread. Mindful meditation might help a person face drowning with equanimity, but it would do absolutely nothing to right the *Titanic*, he said. It wasn't individual efforts to achieve inner peace, it wasn't a compassionate attitude toward others that might have led to timely preventative action, but rather a collective, fanatical, over-the-top obsession with impending doom.

It was useless, the man said, to deny that suffering of immense magnitude lay ahead, or that there'd be any escaping it.

How, then, should we live?

One thing we should start asking ourselves was whether or not we should go on having children.

(Here, the discomposure I mentioned earlier: murmurs and shifting among the audience, that woman's nervous laugh. Also, this part was new. The subject of children had not been raised in the magazine article.)

To be clear, he was not saying that every woman expecting a child should consider having an abortion, the man said. Of course he was not saying that. What he was saying was that perhaps the idea of planning families in the way that people had been doing for generations needed to be rethought. He was saying that perhaps it was a mistake to bring human beings into a world that had such a strong possibility of becoming, in their lifetimes, a bleak and terrifying if not wholly unlivable place. He was asking whether to go ahead blindly and behave as if there was little or no such possibility might not be selfish, and perhaps even immoral, and cruel.

And, after all, he said, weren't there already countless children in the world desperate for protection from already existing threats? Weren't there millions upon millions of people suffering from various humanitarian crises that millions upon millions of other people simply chose to forget? Why could we not turn our attention to the teeming sufferers already in our midst?

And here, perhaps, was a last chance for us to redeem ourselves, the man raised his voice to say. The only moral, meaningful course for a civilization facing its own end: To learn how to ask forgiveness and to atone in some tiny measure for the devastating harm we had done to our human family and to our fellow creatures and to the beautiful earth. To love and forgive one another as best we could. And to learn how to say goodbye.

The man took his iPad from the lectern and walked swiftly backstage. You could hear from the rhythm of the clapping that people were confused. Was that it? Was he coming back? But it was the woman who had introduced him who now reappeared on the podium, thanked everyone for coming, and wished us all good night.

And then we were on our feet and moving herdishly out of the auditorium, spilling out of the building, into the crisp night air. Which, in spite of it being so far one of the warmest years on record, was, just now, the perfect seasonable temperature for that month in that part of the world.

I need a drink, a voice near me said. To which: Me too!

There was a subdued aura about the departing crowd. Some people looked dazed and were silent. Others remarked on the lack of a Q&A. That's so arrogant, said one. Maybe he was miffed because it wasn't a full house, said another.

I heard: What a bore.

And: It was *your* idea to come to this thing, not mine.

An elderly man at the center of a knot of other elderly people was making them all laugh. Oy! *It's over, it's over, it's ohhhh-ver.* I thought it was Roy Orbison up there.

I heard: Melodramatic . . . Irresponsible.

And: Totally right, every word.

And (furiously): Will you please tell me, what was the fucking *point*?

I quickened my pace, leaving the crowd behind, but walking almost in step with me was a man I recognized from the audience. He was wearing a dark suit, running shoes, and a baseball cap. He was alone, and as he walked he was whistling, of all tunes, "My Favorite Things."

I need a drink. To be honest, I'd been thinking the same thing well before I heard someone say it. I wanted a drink before going back to the apartment, before going to bed. I had decided to walk back from the campus, as I had walked there (it was less than a mile), and I knew that along the way I'd be passing several places where a drink—a glass of wine was what I wanted—could be had. But I was a stranger in that town and unsure where, if anywhere, I'd be comfortable having a drink by myself.

Every place I looked was too crowded or too noisy or seemed, for some other reason, uninviting. A feeling of loneliness and disappointment came over me. It was a familiar feeling. I thought of a woman I knew who had started carrying her own flask. I was ready to give up when I remembered that there was a café on the corner of my host's street that had been empty when I passed it earlier and where, I had noticed, wine was served.

Now, of course, the café was not empty. But from the

street I could see that, though all the tables seemed to be taken, there were places to sit at the bar.

I went in and sat down. I had a moment's panic because the bartender, a young man with the kind of ornate tattoos and facial hair that make me think of a conversation piece, ignored me, even though he was not just then attending to anyone else. I took out my phone, that reliable prop, and spent a few moments tickling it.

Raindrops on roses and whiskers on kittens.

At last the bartender sauntered over (so I had not become see-through) and took my order. At last I had my drink. Red wine: one of *my* favorite things. It would be easier, with a glass, to gather my thoughts, after a long hard day that had given me much to think about. But immediately I was distracted by a conversation taking place at a table right behind me. Two people whom, unless I turned around, I couldn't see. I did not turn around. But I soon got the gist of their story.

A father and daughter. The mother was dead. She had died a year ago after a long struggle with an illness. They were a Jewish family. The time had come for the unveiling. The daughter had traveled from somewhere out of town for the ceremony. The father kept his voice low, just above a mumble. The daughter spoke louder and louder until—partly because for some reason the bartender kept turning up the music—she was almost shouting.

It was so hard for your mother.

I know, Dad.

What she went through.

I know. I was there.

She was brave, though. But no one could be that brave.

I know, Dad, I was there. I was there the whole time. In fact, that's something I was hoping we could talk about. You remember how it was, Dad. I was the one taking care of everything. You were so worried about Mom, she was so worried about you. I understand how hard it was for both of you.

I remember how hard it was for her.

I was hoping we could talk about this, Dad. I was going through so much myself then—nobody really knew. You and Mom were there for each other, and I was there for both of you. But no one was there for me. It was like my own needs had to be pushed aside, and we've never really dealt with that part of it. My therapist says it's why I'm having so many problems.

(*Inaudible.*)

I know, Dad. But what I'm saying is that it was hard for me, too, and it's still hard for me, and I need for that to be acknowledged. All this time, and it's still going on, still impacting my life every day. My therapist says it has to be dealt with.

I thought the service went well. What did you think of the service?

When I arrived back at my host's apartment, I found her at the kitchen table with a mug of tea.

I saw you, she said—stumping me.

At the lecture, she said. I saw you there.

Oh, I said. I didn't see you.

You were in the back, she said, but I was way up front. I was with a friend of mine, and she always likes to sit close. I saw you when we were leaving. Did you stop somewhere to get something to eat?

Yes, I lied, feeling ridiculous. Was it because I was ashamed to say that I'd stopped for a drink? In fact, I had not been able to eat at all since leaving the hospital that day, because of what I had seen—and smelled—there.

She offered to make me some tea, which I declined.

I don't know about you, she said, but I really did not like that man. My friend was the one who said we should go hear him, because she's a big fan. Honestly, if we hadn't been sitting right under his nose, I think I might've got up and left. I mean, I know he's a big intellectual and all, with important things to say, but I think tone matters, and his tone really bugged me. And I'm not saying he isn't right about how bad things are—I tremble for my grandchildren's future, believe me—but to talk like that, like there's no hope, I don't know, that just seems wrong to me. I don't think anyone has the right to tell people there's no hope. You can't just get up and tell people there's no hope! And it doesn't make sense. He thinks you can take away people's hope and then expect them to—what did he say?—love and take care of each other? Like, how is that going to happen.

I agreed that this was a good point.

And can you imagine, she said, if people ever really got so hopeless about life that they stopped having kids? Sounds like something from a dystopian novel. In fact, I'm sure I read that in a book somewhere. Or maybe it was that the state had made getting pregnant a crime. I forget. Anyway, I can't believe he's serious. Telling people to stop having kids. Who the hell is he?

He was my ex. But I didn't say that.

And did you notice, she said, even though it was a campus event, there were almost no young people there?

I had noticed.

I guess it's not really their thing, she said.

Well, I can't say it wasn't an interesting way to spend an evening, she said. What did you think?

I agreed that it was an interesting way to spend an evening.

Are you sure you don't want some tea? Anything? A glass of wine?

No, that's all right, thanks, I said.

Before I went to my room, it occurred to me to tell her about the man who'd left the talk whistling "My Favorite Things."

Oh, that's hilarious, she said. She had a sharp, tooting laugh. I never liked that sappy song, but I do know all the words.

And so, in yet another of that day's odd moments, I stood

in the kitchen of a strange house listening to a woman I
didn't know sing all the words to "My Favorite Things."

In bed, about to turn out the light, I picked up the topmost
book from the stack of mysteries on the nightstand. *A psychological thriller in the tradition of Highsmith and Simenon, set in
the seamy noirish world of seventies New York.*

   A man is plotting to kill his wife. He and she have not
been married very long, and, except for a brief period of sexual infatuation after they first met, he has never really cared
for her. Believably enough, given that she is mean and selfish
and treats him with contempt, the man has come to hate her.
Misogyny has always run deep in this man, partly thanks
to a mother who enjoyed beating him when he was small.
It seems he has never had sex with any woman—from the
town prostitute he frequents to his lawful wedded wife—
without experiencing intense shame. Beginning in childhood, with his own mother, he has often fantasized about
murdering this or that particular woman. In his mind he
dubs these women "candidates." For strangulation, that is.

   The man has arranged to take his wife on a second honeymoon to the Caribbean resort where they'd spent their first
one. He chooses the resort hotel for the scene of the crime because he figures it will be quite easy to fake a break-in from
the balcony of their room. The "burglar" will find his wife
alone and end up strangling her. The man plans every detail
with scrupulous care, then sits back to wait for the day of

their departure, set for some months away. In the meantime, though, he detects certain changes in his wife's behavior that he is unsure how to interpret. He becomes convinced that she is hiding something, something that might foil his plan. As it turns out, the wife's secret is that she'd become pregnant. The man learns this at the same time that he learns that she has just had an abortion. A Catholic—albeit a lapsed one—the wife becomes obsessed with the idea that she is going to Hell.

The man can hardly believe his luck. No need to travel all the way to Aruba. No need to fake breaking and entering. Best of all, no need to wait. His wife has just handed him a wholly believable reason for her to take her own life. He has even overheard her crying to her best friend about her fear that, in the eyes of the Church, she is guilty of murder. And so the man begins to work out details of a new plan.

But before the murder can take place, the wife springs another surprise, running off with a boyfriend whose existence the man had never even suspected. At this, the man turns raging beast. He drives straight to the house of the prostitute and strangles her, then strangles her pimp, who happens to be watching television in the next room. Later he thinks that, although killing the woman had given him the big rush and release he'd been seeking, it was killing another man that made him feel proud. Later still, he reflects on his feelings about killing the woman: He'd had nothing against her. He didn't think she deserved to die. But he didn't feel bad for her, either. She was a whore, and whores got murdered all the time. It was one of the things whores were for.

Thus ends part one.

Patricia Highsmith once admitted that she liked criminals, finding this type of person extremely interesting and even admirable for their vitality, freedom of spirit, and refusal to bow down to anyone. But the criminals in most crime fiction are not like that. Especially the killers, most especially the serial killers, are not like that. This one has the familiar one-dimensional personality of the violent psychopath. He is brutal and sadistic, lacking in conscience and empathy. What makes him somewhat more sympathetic is that he has a yearning for self-improvement. Still in his twenties, he is gripped by the idea that he has somehow missed out on some very significant part of life, which he connects to an understanding and appreciation of the arts. When the novel opens, it's a beautiful summer dusk, and the man has been hanging out by himself at the gleaming, brand-new complex of Lincoln Center. He sees rainbows in the jets of the plaza's central fountain and watches enviously as people stream toward the various performances, a thing that he not only has never done but has trouble even picturing himself doing. He may be plotting a barbaric crime, but he is also fantasizing about "getting more culture." Later, the same yearning impels him to sneak into classes at Columbia University. Getting more culture, reading big books, learning about music and art—this is how he hopes to spend more time once he's got uxoricide out of his system. This aspect of the killer's character did not make me like him. But it did make me feel for him. I had the sense that, as much as his sins, this virtue would have a role in bringing him down.

I was perfectly happy not to find out, though. I was happy to leave the story there, after thirty-odd pages, at the end of part one. I didn't have much curiosity about how the murders would be solved. It never matters to me how a mystery ends. In fact, I have found that, after so many pages of so many twists and turns and other to-do, the ending is usually something of a letdown, and the bad guy being caught and ultimately brought to justice or destroyed is invariably the least exciting part of the plot.

I like the story of a nursing home resident who had one book, one whodunit, that she was able to read over and over as though it were new. By the time she finished it she would've forgotten everything that came before, and as she started reading again she would forget how it all turned out.

My host has hearing loss. She did not hear me come into the living room though I made no attempt to be quiet. It was the following morning, I was ready to leave, and I'd come to thank her and say goodbye. She did not see me because she was standing at the window, looking out. When I spoke she spun around with a gasp, hand on heart.

It happens to some women after a certain age that something babyish comes back into the face. The flesh has fattened and slackened at the same time, and you can see what the woman must have looked like as a toddler. So the woman looked to me just then: like a frightened toddler. I cannot say how much this impression was heightened by the fact that she was crying.

Of course she was all right, she said, tooting a laugh. There was nothing wrong, she said, nothing at all. I was just, well, you know. I was just thinking.

Imagine my surprise (he wrote) to see you in the audience last night. Have you moved? I had no idea. I suppose if you'd wanted to talk to me you'd have looked for me afterward. I suppose if you'd wanted to be seen you wouldn't have sat way in the back. Anyway, I did want you to know that I saw you and to thank you for coming. I thought of trying to reach you after dinner, but it went on quite late. I thought maybe if you were willing to get up very early we could have breakfast at my hotel before I had to leave. Then it occurred to me that the very idea of having breakfast with me might fill you with horror. Well, too late now. I'm at the airport. Again, thanks for coming. It made a difference to me, up there, knowing that you were listening. I hope all's well with you and that you won't mind my sending this message. I worry that it might give you pain, and yet it seemed the right thing to do. But, needless to say, please don't feel that you have to reply.

————

What gave me pain was seeing him so much older. Not that he'd ever been handsome, but still. The only thing harder than seeing yourself grow old is seeing the people you've loved grow old.

She was just thinking, she said.

Flaubert said, To think is to suffer.

Is this the same as Aristotle's To perceive is to suffer?

Always make the audience suffer as much as possible. Alfred Hitchcock.

Sufferin' succotash. Sylvester the cat.

II

The cancer treatments my friend had been receiving—and which included one course that was still experimental—succeeded beyond what cautious doctors had allowed her to hope.

She was going to live.

Or rather, as she put it, she was not going to die.

Actually, what she said was *I don't have to leave the party just yet.*

Now she was swinging between euphoria and depression. Euphoria for the obvious reason; depression because, well, she wasn't exactly sure why, but she'd been warned to expect it.

It sounds absurd, she said. But after thinking all this time that this was the end, and trying to prepare myself for it, survival feels anticlimactic.

In fact, her first thought upon receiving her diagnosis had been that she wouldn't accept any treatment at all. When she learned the survival rate for someone with her type of cancer at the stage at which hers had been found (fifty-fifty, according to her research, though her oncologist would not be pinned down), she foresaw a long period of painful and debilitating treatment during which she would be too sick to do anything that could properly be called living and that, in all likelihood, would fail to save her anyway. She had seen it happen too often, she said. So had I. So had we all. Still, we urged her not to give in, we insisted that she must do everything possible to fight the disease. Fifty-fifty: not the *worst* odds.

And, in the end, it had not been hard to persuade her. She didn't want to leave the party early. And why not be a guinea pig (over her doctor's repeated objections, she kept calling herself that).

Only one person did not try to change her mind. Her daughter said simply: It's your choice.

When I heard this I had a sinking feeling. The two women had a fraught history. Enough bones of contention between us, my friend joked, to make a whole skeleton. She often joked about her relationship with her daughter, partly because humor had always been a strong feature of her personality and partly because it was her way of dealing with difficulty. I remember when her daughter was born: an unusually troubled pregnancy ending in a grueling labor with postpartum hemorrhaging severe enough to require a transfusion—*I guess that's what happens when you bring a monster into the world* was how she'd joke about it later.

They lived two thousand miles apart, and although on speaking terms at the time of my friend's diagnosis (unlike the many times I could recall when they were not), they had not had much contact in years.

I've never even met the man she lives with, my friend told me. I wouldn't be surprised to hear only after the fact that they'd got married.

It's your choice. It wasn't for me to judge this response. No need to put the cruelest and most sinister connotation on it, either. But I knew how it might sound to my friend and how much pain it could cause her.

Unnatural is a word that keeps coming to mind when I think about this mother and daughter. For as long as I can remember, there seemed to be only misunderstanding between them. Instances of affection were rare enough when they shared the same roof. Once the daughter moved out, they vanished altogether.

When my friend began a sentence *If I had known how it would be,* I was certain that she'd go on: I would never have had a child. But *I would have tried to have at least one more* was what she actually said.

Once upon a time, faced with a child that mystified or repelled because of some trait—illness or disability, lack of affection, bad behavior—parents were only too willing to believe that their real child had been stolen and that the thieves (according to many folklores, most likely devils or fairies) had left a replacement that was really a troll or a devilkin or some other nonhuman thing. Imagine how many times the myth of the changeling has been justification for child abuse: corporal punishment, neglect, abandonment, infanticide even.

Any notion that my friend's daughter might have been accidentally switched at birth was easily scotched: She had her mother's fine blue eyes down to the gold rings around the pupils. The same heart-shaped face, the same bowed legs, voices that couldn't be told apart. But I remember hearing my friend say it more than once: If we were living in the Dark Ages, I'd swear the kid was a changeling.

When pressed, an exasperated sigh. She just doesn't *feel* like mine.

Which never failed to chill me.

And when she made the comment—if she'd known how things would turn out she'd have tried to have another child—that too chilled me. But I thought I understood. If she'd had another child, and if she succeeded in having a better relationship with it, wouldn't that prove that it wasn't all her fault how badly things had turned out with her daughter? I understood. Or, at least, I tried to.

She would also insist that everything would have been different—meaning better—if her daughter had been a son.

This is the saddest story I have ever heard, begins one of the twentieth century's most famous novels. Often this comes to mind when I hear people talk about their messy lives, especially about their unhappy families.

There was a father, of course. Or rather the ghost of one. They'd been in the same crowd all through high school, and at the end, briefly, just before he was drafted into the army, a couple. When he returned from the war they had tried but failed to make a go of it. The daughter had been, my friend confessed, the result of break-up sex.

We knew it was over, she said. But we weren't angry with each other, and I had no idea when I was going to have sex again. It was me who insisted on one last time.

The thought of marriage never entered her mind, she said. She was not in love with him, she had never been in love with him—besides nostalgia for high school they had no interests in common—and she had no desire to have this man in her life for years to come. When she told him she was pregnant, she also made it clear that she expected nothing from him. She had wealthy parents, who, as it happened, were more delighted than upset to learn of their daughter's condition. They had always regretted not having been able to have more than one child themselves. Whatever the circumstances, the promise of a grandchild was cause for celebration.

And since my friend's boyfriend had returned from the war feeling lost and unsure of just about everything except that he was not ready for fatherhood, he was all for a plan that subtracted him from the story. In any case, he longed to leave his hometown and start a new life elsewhere. He didn't even wait for the baby to be born before taking off.

A decade of silence ended with news of his death. One day, he and his wife happened to be out driving in the country when they came upon a house whose second floor was in flames and from which, the wife later explained, her husband said he'd heard screaming. He had run into the house and up the stairs and then, overcome by the heat and smoke, suffered cardiac arrest. Firefighters arriving just minutes later were unable to revive him. As for the screams, the wife herself had heard nothing, she said, and it turned out that, at the time of the fire, no one was home.

I should never have told her that story, my friend said. I should've pretended all along that I had no idea who her father was.

In the mother's eyes, the father, insignificant enough to begin with, had diminished with time to practically nothing. For the daughter, absence had only made him loom ever larger, and in death he became a colossus.

Strikingly handsome—see the high school yearbook. (*You'd have expected him to be with someone a lot prettier* was one of the sharper arrows in the daughter's quiver.) A soldier: brave, romantic. A hero who'd sacrificed his life to save strangers from a burning house. A man like that doesn't simply abandon his own child. And yet she had never met him. She had never even spoken with him.

And whose fault was that?

It broke her heart, said my friend, when she was cleaning out her daughter's closet one day and found the letters she'd been secretly writing him.

And in which, it seemed, she had poured out all her resentment against mother and grandparents.

I know they didn't give you a chance. I know what my mother is like and what she's capable of doing to get her own way.

She hated being the child of a single mother—the only such among her friends when she was growing up. She could never shake her feelings of shame for her fatherlessness. Equally lasting was her hostility toward anyone her mother dated. Though she would never marry, my friend had affairs with several men while her daughter was growing up, and with every one of them the girl had behaved as rudely as possible. It would not be unfair to say that she helped drive some away.

She hated growing up in her grandparents' house as if she and her mother were siblings. (To be honest, said my friend, I left a lot of the child rearing to my mother, which was how Mom wanted it too, and I really did feel more like an older sister than like a mother myself.) The daughter could not tolerate seeing how well mother and grandparents got along. She was an alien among them, *her father's daughter*, not like any of her mother's people, with whom she could not get along at all.

I will never forgive that woman for coming between us.

That woman of course being me, my friend said.

Love letters was what they were.

She had managed to turn him into a great passion, my friend said. She would've sold the rest of us into bondage to spend one hour with him.

And that's what bothers me most, she said. Okay, hate *me*. I'm the one who got knocked up and said no to a shotgun marriage, I'm the terrible mother. But what about my parents? All they ever did was love and take care of her, and she made what should have been their golden years miserable. That's what *I'll* never forgive.

If she'd known how things would turn out, she'd have tried to give them another grandchild.

This is the saddest story I have ever heard.

In middle school, she wrote a poem about her father that included the lines "I was the one in the burning house / I was the one you heard screaming."

All about what a tragedy her whole life was, her mother described it. This much-loved, much-wanted child who grew up with every conceivable privilege in a world full of suffering, and here she is, acting like she's an orphan, a refugee, a goddamn boat person. She even had the nerve to call herself that.

"I am an emotional boat person" was another line from the poem.

Her grandparents had also been upset by the poem, in

which they were accused of being unfeeling rich snobs, more enemies than loving family.

It was the last fucking straw, my friend said. And then the school went and gave it a *prize*!

Might as well disclose it here: I never had much sympathy for the daughter. I never liked her. She was, it must be said, an extraordinarily unlikable little girl. I recall how guilty my aversion to her used to make me feel: she was just a child, after all. But I had never before met a child so disagreeable. She lied with the skill of a con artist. She broke her toys on purpose. She stole things that she could have had just by asking for them. She bullied smaller children. When her grandmother gave her a kitten she teased it so relentlessly that it became almost feral.

When it came time for college, she applied only to schools in distant states (She wants to get as far away from me as possible, her mother said, accurately), and later, for postgraduate work, she went farther still and lived for a few years abroad. She had always shown both a gift and a passion for writing, but rather than pursue a literary career (Follow in *my* footsteps? said my friend. Never happen), she went into business, specifically the business of advising others how to manage their businesses, eventually specializing in hospitality and entertainment. At this she turned out to be something of a whiz, and because it was work that involved a lot of travel, and travel was the one thing she loved more than work itself, and because, thanks to her job, travel usually meant complimentary luxury travel, she had turned out to be happier than we who'd known her as a girl would ever have predicted.

Once she'd established her complete independence from them, her hostility toward her family diminished. Her grandparents' deaths, which fell one right after the other, triggered feelings of remorse of which her mother had come to fear she was incapable. It would be an exaggeration to say that mother and daughter reconciled—there would never be true peace between them—but there was less tension, and for a few years, at least, they managed to be in each other's lives in a manner resembling a normal family relationship.

But it was too late. There was too much history, too much bad blood between them. (With typical dysfunctional-family logic, my friend easily forgave her parents for voting Republican but not her daughter, ever.) In the end, it was simply easier to let go, to do without each other. Just as my friend had yet to meet the man her daughter was living with, her daughter had no idea that her mother also had been seeing someone (a man whose interest cooled, however, once it was clear that she might be seriously ill).

This is where things stood at the time of my friend's diagnosis.

It's your choice. What a thing to say, my friend said. It's your choice. Period. Like it was a small thing. Like it had nothing to do with her.

I held her hand, I tried to soothe her. I said, People say
the wrong things—

You were smart not to have children, she said.

It was not, by any means, the first time she'd said this to
me, but this time it was said with unusual force. Then, as if
realizing that maybe she ought not to have spoken so to me:
You know, I specifically told other people not to come see me
this afternoon because I wanted it to be just us.

I did not have any real news to share so I talked about
other things, the usual things, books I'd been reading, movies I'd seen, and how everyone who lived in my building
was freaking out because one apartment was reported to
have bedbugs. My friend and I had met in our early twenties
when we worked at the same literary journal. The editor in
chief, our old boss, had died earlier that year, and we talked
about him, about our old days at the journal and what its
future might be, now that its founder and editor in chief was
gone, and I told her about the memorial service, which I'd
attended, and which she said that she, too, would have attended had she not been ill.

We talked about other people we knew in common, others we'd first met at the journal, the ones with whom we
were still friends, the ones with whom we'd lost touch. The
dead. I worried about all this talk about death, some of it
about people (like our old boss) who'd succumbed to the
same disease now threatening my friend's life, but it was she

who directed the conversation, as she pretty much always did when we were together: it was her way.

Though she was somewhat groggy from medication (and, though she denied it, I believe also in pain), she carried on in the emphatic manner she was known for, unmistakably someone who'd spent a good part of her life behind a lectern. I was reminded that she had always been known for her vigor. She was the kind of person whom others describe as a fighter, a survivor, and it was because of this that we who knew her were surprised when she announced that she intended to forgo treatment. And unsurprised when she changed her mind. She had not been wrong, however, to dread treatment. At first I hardly recognized her. *White as an egg and skinny as a chopstick* was how she'd tried to prepare me. And minus every strand of what had once been a thundercloud of hair.

About an hour into my visit we were interrupted by her oncologist, a youthful and classically handsome brown man, like a movie star cast as the hero doctor, and I was touched to see how she flirted with him (and how he, subtly, good-naturedly, flirted back) before I was asked to step out of the room. A private room. (You won't believe what this is costing, she told me, but I couldn't bear the idea of lying here all day with some roommate watching TV or gabbing on the phone. I can't stand it even for a few minutes in the lounge. And I, in turn, told her about being in the hospital overnight for minor surgery the year before, and how I'd had to listen for hours to the woman in the next bed phoning updates on her condition to an endless series of people, including her hairdresser, and, weirdly enough, one apparently bewildered person to whom she had to explain how it was that they even knew each other.)

After her doctor had finished his consultation we picked up where we'd left off. Then, all at once, she fell back, exhausted. It was that sudden, as though she'd been shot. She no longer had the energy to talk, but she asked me to stay a bit longer. A nurse came to take blood and my friend snapped at her, I no longer remember what, ostensibly, for. (I don't like that one was all she said later.) The nurse, the picture of professional poise, winked at me as she went out. They are trained to forgive, in cancer care.

I'm so glad you came, my friend said when I kissed her goodbye.

I told her I'd come again, the next day.

What are you doing tonight? Anything?

I told her I was going to hear my ex give a talk.

Oh, *him*, she said. And she rolled her eyes.

I asked if she'd read the article on which the talk was based and she said that she had.

Nice to see he's still his old ball-of-fun self, she said.

Recently a story appeared in an anthology, based on a true story familiar to my friend and me because it involved someone we used to know, another old coworker. A man teaching at a university was overcome by the presence in one of his classes of a young man who happened to remind him of the beautiful ephebe who'd been the love and obsession of his youth. Giving in to temptation, he seduced the student and was thrilled when his feelings were returned. A passionate romance ensued, with both men hoping that, despite the generational difference in their ages, their relationship would endure. But after a short time it was revealed that the young man was in fact the professor's former lover's son. This discovery set off a series of deep disturbances in the professor's psyche. He immediately broke off the relationship but was never able to get back to a normal life, becoming so distraught that in the end he killed himself.

I remember that, at the time, what none of us could quite believe was that, until the truth was revealed, this man had managed to ignore not only the clue of the family resemblance, which was in fact striking, but the much bigger clue that his two lovers *shared the same surname.* Also incredible, that he never once mentioned anything about either of these remarkable "coincidences" to the student, and apparently never sought to learn whether there might be something more behind them.

The power of denial. It's happened more than once: a girl finds herself giving birth, in a high school bathroom, say, and later reveals that she'd had no idea she was pregnant, the many changes taking place in her body having been attributed by her to—whatever.

The boundless capacity of the human mind for self-delusion: my ex was certainly not wrong about that.

In the published story, which was written by the young (well, no longer young) lover, characters' genders and other details have been changed so that the student with whom the professor ends up having an affair turns out to be a daughter about whose existence he'd never been told. According to the writer, this was to create a more dramatic conflict and to make the suicide more convincing. Of course, the truth was far more interesting, and my friend was not the only one who felt that the writer had in fact "ruined" the story—forgetting that what had actually happened was not a work of fiction. Some people who were close to the professor were upset to see him turned into a fictional character and thought the story should never have been written or published at all.

But there it is, and now we have it. Another saddest story.

Jesus, du weisst is the title of an Austrian documentary I saw about fifteen years ago and have never got out of my head. *Jesus, You Know.* Six Catholics are shown, each alone in a different empty church, having agreed to pray aloud while kneeling and facing the camera that has been set up on a tripod in the chancel. These ordinary believers, three men and three women, have a lot on their chests, they have a lot on their minds, there is oh so much that they want to tell Jesus about. The phrase "you know" is repeated several times. (In fact, *You Know, Jesus* would have been the more accurate title, since it's the informal conversation filler and not the Lord's omniscience that is the meaning here.) These intimate one-sided talks, mostly about family problems, are more like something you'd expect to hear a person telling a shrink or a confessor than what comes to mind at the word *prayer.* Not quite the love letter to God, not the raising of the heart and mind to God or the requesting of good things from him as defined by the Catholic Church.

One woman is depressed because her husband has suffered a stroke and now spends all his time watching bad TV shows. Another complains of a husband who's cheating on her. Maybe, with Jesus' help, she can find the right words to make an anonymous call to inform the other woman's husband. And might Jesus also give her the strength not to murder her husband with the poison that she confesses already to have obtained.

An elderly man emotionlessly questions Jesus about the abuse inflicted on him when he was a child: Why did my father beat me. Why did my mother spit in my face.

A young man goes from bemoaning his parents' failure to understand his religious devotion to describing his bewildering and sometimes religious erotic fantasies.

A young couple takes turns discussing the unhappiness that has arisen in their relationship because she wants one thing in life and he wants quite another thing.

They drone on and on, the six. There is no other way to put it. As there is no way to ignore the fact that a considerable amount of what we hear from them would have to be called whining. A defensive tone creeps in: each person seems to have felt a pressing need to explain his or her feelings, to present his or her situation as though laying out a case before a judge.

Of the handful of people who were in the audience with me, not everyone stayed till the end.

What the prayers recorded in the film lay bare are depths of loneliness, self-doubt, and sadness. Each supplicant seems to be crying out for love—a love they've never found or a love they fear they're on the verge of losing. Although the people in the film are of different ages and come from different backgrounds, they share two most important things: religion and nationality. What would happen if the director's experiment were to be repeated with other groups of believers, non-Austrians, non-Catholics—would the results be the same? I think so. Watching the film, hearing the prayers, I felt like a witness to the human condition.

What is prayer and is God even listening are two questions the filmmaker wants the viewer/voyeur to chew on. Me, I left the theater thinking of the popular inspirational command: Be kind, because everyone you meet is going through a struggle.

Often attributed to Plato.

Not long after I saw the documentary, I happened to catch an interview on the radio with the filmmaker John Waters. Asked to make some movie recommendations, he immediately named *Jesus, You Know*. My favorite holiday movie, he called it (we were in the Christmas season). The people are *maddening*, John Waters said. And what the movie makes clear is that, if there really was a Supreme Being who had to listen to people's prayers all the time, he would go out of his mind.

III

I went to the gym. I have been going to the same neighborhood gym for many years. Others have been going there
for at least as long as I have so I see some of the same people whenever I'm there. One person in particular I wonder
about: all these years, no matter what day or what hour I go,
this woman is there. Though we've never become friends—
if we ever even exchanged names, I've forgotten hers—we
tend to chat if we happen to be in the locker room at the
same time. I remember our first conversation was about the
book *Infinite Jest*, a copy of which she happened to have with
her. When I asked her how she liked it she said that the best
thing about it was its length. She would be reading the book
for a long time, she said. Weeks. And she felt that, even if
she didn't love it, at least she'd be getting her money's worth.

(I could not help thinking of an all-day lollipop.) She was so tired, this woman said, of paying twenty bucks for short books—stuff that lasted only a short time, sometimes not even a weekend.

And sometimes it's just a book of poems, she said. How can they charge that much for a book of poems? Who buys them?

Not many people, I assured her.

At the time, the woman at the gym was young, still in school, as I recall, or maybe just out of school. Art school. I remember very clearly what she looked like because she was so pretty, with features that were vivid and dramatic even without a touch of makeup, and how I was reminded of a story about a movie director saying about a child actress that she shouldn't be filmed wearing all that makeup, only to be told that little Elizabeth Taylor wasn't wearing any makeup.

The woman at the gym was also blessed with what would have been a great body even without all the effort she spent working out. Over time, though, her looks have changed, I wouldn't say drastically but more than most people's do. In middle age she is toned but overweight, her precise features have blurred, the dazzle is gone. No one is more aware of this than she is. In the locker room she sits hunched and swathed in towels with a look of grievance on her face. Why do they have to have all these *mirrors* in here, why do the lights have to be this fucking *bright*?

I agree about the lights. They are fucking bright. But her

remark about the mirrors confuses me. I have no trouble ignoring them.

How was it possible, the woman in the locker room wanted to know, for a person to work out every day and watch every bite she ate and still not lose weight. She now ate half of what she used to eat, she said, but every year she had to eat less just to keep from becoming a blimp. At this rate, she'd soon be down to a carrot and a hard-boiled egg a day. And it wouldn't be so bad if it didn't hurt, she said, but when her stomach was empty it was like a rat trying to gnaw its way out of there, at night sometimes it was so bad that she couldn't sleep. She knew it sounded crazy, the woman in the locker room said, but when her sister got cancer and lost thirty pounds she couldn't help wishing it would happen to her. And was it so crazy? After all, always hating the way she looked, always fighting against her own body and always, always losing the battle meant that she was depressed all the time, more depressed than her sister had been about getting cancer. And anyway her sister was fine now.

Shopping for clothes, the woman in the locker room went on. That used to be *fun*. That used to bring *joy*. But now it was more like a punishment. Whenever she needed new pants or a new dress, she had to try on a hundred things before she found something that fit, and the whole time she had to look in the mirror. She would stand there looking at herself in the mirror and gritting her teeth, she said, gritting her teeth now as she told me the story, thinking how it used to be—not just how much fun but the high she always got from admiring her own body.

From the back is the worst, she said. I really can't stand how I look from the back. I never wear anything anymore that doesn't cover my butt.

Going to the beach, going swimming, getting a tan—all these things used to be fun too, the woman in the locker room said. But now there was no way she'd ever appear in public in a swimsuit, she wouldn't even go out wearing shorts. No matter how hot it was, she said, she always covered herself up. Even if she lost weight, even if she was thin again, she wouldn't show her body in public, she said. Even though she knew she didn't look worse than most women her age—she knew that in fact she looked better than most of them—she didn't understand how some women could show themselves basically naked the way so many did, without self-consciousness, without shame. When she saw a woman walking on the beach with cottage-cheese thighs and a belly slung like a hammock, she had to turn away, the woman in the locker room said, she couldn't even look. *And she would rather die than give anyone a reason to feel that way about her.*

There was genuine horror in the woman's voice. There was horror and bitterness and pain. What a nasty trick life had played on her.

Have you heard the one about X, Y, or Z, who had so

many facelifts that the dimple in her chin is really her na-
vel? As I recall, the first time I heard this joke it was about
Elizabeth Taylor.

Long before the arrival of FaceApp, I remember once hearing someone say that everybody, sometime in their youth—
say around when they finished high school—should be given
digitally altered images showing how they'll probably look
in ten, twenty, fifty years. That way, this person said, at least
they could be prepared. Because most people are in denial
about aging, just as they are about dying. Though they see it
happening all around them, though the example of parents
and grandparents might be right under their nose, they don't
take it in, they don't really believe it will happen to them. It
happens to others, it happens to everyone else, but it won't
happen to them.

But I myself have always thought of this as a blessing.
Youth burdened with full knowledge of just how sad and
painful aging is I would not call youth at all.

The other day, this happened: I was sitting with some
friends at a sidewalk café. A middle-aged woman standing
near the curb was speaking into her phone, her voice raised
above the street noise. I'm the youngest, we heard her say.
From the window of a passing car, a man roared: How can
you be the youngest? You look a hundred years old!

An elderly and once very beautiful woman I know had
this to say on the subject: In our culture, what you look like is

such an important part of who you are and how people treat
you. Especially if you're female. So if you're good-looking,
if you're a good-looking girl or woman, you get used to a
certain level of attention. You get used to admiration—not
just from people you know but from strangers, from almost
everyone. You get used to compliments, you get used to people wanting you around, wanting to give you things and to
do things for you. You get used to inspiring love. If you're really good-looking and you aren't mentally ill or obnoxiously
conceited or a total dimwit, you get so used to being popular,
you get so used to love and admiration that you take it for
granted, you don't even know how privileged you are. Then
one day it all disappears. Actually, it happens gradually. You
begin to notice certain things. Heads no longer turn when
you pass by, people you meet don't always later remember
your face. And this becomes your new life, your strange new
life: an ordinary, undesirable person with a common, forget-
table face.

I think of this sometimes, the once beautiful woman said,
when I hear young women complain about how, wherever
they go, guys leer at them or make catcalls—all that coarse,
unwanted attention. And I get it, she said, because I used
to feel that way too. But show me the girl who'll be saying
years from now, Sing hallelujah, I'm so glad that never happens to me anymore! It's like menopause, she said. No matter
how much of a relief it might be not to have to deal with

menstruation anymore, show me the woman who greets her first missed period with joy.

I remember, the elderly and once beautiful woman said, after I reached a certain age it was like a bad dream—one of those nightmares where for some reason no one you know recognizes you anymore. People didn't seek me out or try to make friends with me the way they'd always done before. I'd never been in the position of having to work at making people like and admire me. Suddenly I was all shy and socially awkward. Worse, I started to feel paranoid. Had I turned into one of those pathetic people always trying to get others to like them when everyone knows that that's just the sort of person other people never do like?

One day my son brought home a friend, the once beautiful woman went on, and I happened to overhear her say, Your mom's kind of weird, isn't she. To this day I'm not sure what the girl meant, I never did get to the bottom of it, but it threw me into a crisis. Around that time I started to withdraw. I mean, I still went to work and took care of my family but I did less and less socializing. Also, though I never got fat, I stopped wearing makeup and I stopped coloring my gray hair.

I remember, the once beautiful woman said, one of the worst parts of it all was the guilt. I honestly felt that, by growing older and losing my looks, I was a disappointment to people, I was letting them down. There was no denying that I was a disappointment to my husband, not that he ever said so, but he didn't hide it, either. And when he started cheating, I knew that he used the fact that I didn't try to make myself look better—meaning, of course, younger—as a justification. My own mother, who once worked as a model and was what you'd call a woman of the world, had warned me that I was putting my marriage at risk. After all, my looks had had everything to do with why my husband married me, it was a big part of what he fell in love with, he and I both knew that, it would have been absurd to deny it. But the girl he fell in love with and married was now gone—and how was he to have known he'd be incapable of desiring the woman in her place? And so he did what so many other men in his predicament do, the once beautiful woman said, he left me for someone else. Someone who, as friends kept pointing out—I suppose because they thought it would make me feel better—bore a strong resemblance to what I had looked like twenty years earlier, when I was her age. Friends also kept telling me, Now you'll meet someone else, now you'll find a man who loves you for yourself and not just for how you look! Funny thing, though, I never did meet such a man.

Maybe I really am *weird*, like the girl said, or maybe I'm just a terrible, shallow person, but it often feels to me as though I had died, the once beautiful woman said. All those years ago I died, and I've been a ghost ever since. I've been mourning my lost self ever since, and nothing, not even my love for my children and grandchildren, can make up for it.

The woman at the gym had always wanted to be a painter, she said on another day when we met in the locker room. I thought I could make it but I wasn't sure, she said, because that's how it is when you're starting out and you haven't had a chance to prove yourself. Most of my teachers were men, she said, and I remember how two in particular really encouraged me. They were always telling me how good I was. Of course, they were also always coming on to me, but that wasn't any surprise, other men came on to me too, and a lot of male teachers came on to their female students back then, that's just how it was. But I couldn't help having doubts. I couldn't be sure if they really liked my work or they just liked me. I couldn't ignore the fact that my one female teacher wasn't as impressed with my work as the men were. But then I thought maybe she was just being competitive or jealous, like a lot of women are, and in fact one of the men assured me that this was definitely the case. The longer this went on, the more confused I got, she said. I didn't know who to trust, I couldn't tell what was sincere, what was flattery. I lost all confidence in my own judgment. I'm not trying to make excuses. If being an artist really had been my destiny, I know nothing should have stopped me. But when I look back I think, My God, those men! They really had me turned around. I couldn't tell what was real anymore.

One day around the time David Foster Wallace killed

himself, I asked the woman at the gym if she remembered that our first conversation had been about *Infinite Jest*. She did not, and she thought I'd made a mistake. She'd heard of the book, but she was pretty sure she hadn't read it. I never read long books like that, she said. Who has the time?

IV

Women's stories are often sad stories.

Like most people past the age of sixty, Woman A often thinks about growing old. At the same time, she often thinks back to those years when old age seemed a very distant thing, more like an option than a law of nature. After graduating from college, she had gone to live in a large city. In those days, rather than look for a husband, or even a steady boyfriend, she was happy to date several different men, and given that she was attractive, fun-loving, and not terribly choosy, this goal was not hard to achieve. Of course, this playing the field wasn't going to last, it wasn't supposed to last (remarkable, in fact, how fast it got old), and she had imagined herself, in due time, settling down with the One. But long before this could happen, now and then when she happened to see a certain type of couple—an elderly woman accompanied by some geezer with rounded shoulders and sparse white flyaway hair, his belt riding high on his ribs—she would feel a sort of ache for the old man she herself was going to end up with one far-off day. That man, as she saw him, though bereft of youth, would still have certain essential things. To begin with, thanks to a long and successful career, he'd have plenty of money to live on. He'd have a good heart, and in spite of the frailties of old age, he'd have his dignity. (It goes without saying he'd have all his marbles.) He and she would live a quiet but stimulating life together, a rich, elegant life, as she saw it: going to concerts and plays and movies, and traveling abroad, though never as part of any god-awful retirees' group tour *please*. Past the age of passion, they would still be romantic, as anyone who saw them, as she did, against the backgrounds of those foreign cities and exotic landscapes could tell. As the years passed, the image of the old man began to appear to her more and more clearly, almost as if he were walking toward her. But as more time passed, his image began, as if walking backward, to recede. And now that she finds herself facing a different old age from the one she used to imagine, the question won't leave her alone. It plays in her head, like something from an old song, or a poem she was forced to memorize in school: Where is the old man? Oh where is the kind, companionable old dear? Could somebody please tell her?

That kind of woman's story.

———

Another story, this one set in Umbria.

. . . where, one summer, Woman B had rented an old farmhouse. Every morning, before it got too hot, she would go for a run in the hills. Most mornings, always at the crest of the same hill, near the remains of a medieval watchtower, she would see the same car parked by the side of the road and the old man to whom it belonged standing nearby, leaning on his cane. The man had a dog, a golden-haired spaniel, that would hurtle furiously barking in her direction whenever she approached. Each time this happened, the old man, failing to remember her from before, would call out, *Signora! Ha paura dei cani?* And each time she would assure him no, she was not afraid of dogs.

The first few mornings, out of courtesy as well as a sense that the old man would probably welcome a bit of attention, she stopped to chat. Her Italian wasn't very good, but since he never remembered her, let alone the substance of their previous conversations, little Italian was needed. She gathered that he was some kind of retired workman and that he had lived all his life in those hills, the descendant of people who had once worked the land belonging to one of the region's castles. She was never sure why he chose to drive always to this particular spot to walk his dog. He himself was too frail to take more than a few cautious steps at a time.

One day, when the air was much heavier than usual, the

woman stripped off the long-sleeved shirt she always wore over her sports bra and tied it around her waist. Just as the old watchtower came into view, the dog came barking toward her. *Ha paura dei cani?* But as she approached she saw that something wasn't right; the man was plainly agitated. She was afraid that maybe the heat had got to him. But a few steps closer and she understood. Indeed, the man made no effort to conceal his lust, eyes raking her half-naked torso, sighing, *Ah, signoraaah*, and lolling out his tongue as if in mimicry of the dog panting at their feet.

She was about to move on when, to her dismay, he let his cane clatter to the ground, and, seizing her bare arm with one hand, began energetically stroking it with his other. A stream of lascivious burbles and grunts poured from his lips. Taking care not to knock him off balance, she managed to wrench herself from his grasp and sprint away.

Easy enough to laugh off the incident, which had been, after all, more comical than anything else. (Like being caught by a satyr, as she would describe it to friends.) But there was also something lingeringly unsettling about it. That she had never felt in any real danger didn't mean there hadn't been an element of violence in his behavior. More troubling, perhaps, was something she saw in his face at the time but did not identify until later: far from being ashamed, the old goat had been proud of his arousal.

Even with the slump of age, he was several inches taller than her and, however weak, still carried considerable bulk.

It wasn't hard to see the powerfully built man he must once have been. Not hard at all to imagine a dangerous and virile young brute capable of seizing a helpless woman he happened to meet in a lonely spot and whom she'd have had no hope of escaping.

It was doubtful that the old man remembered this encounter any better than he'd remembered any previous one. In any case, after that morning she never stopped to speak with him again. Each time she saw him, though, she was struck by the same thought. Here he was, in his eighties at least. No memory, no legs, no wind—yet how the mere sight of a bit of female flesh could knock him off his perch. Surely it had been a while since he'd been capable of fucking. But still. He wanted. He lusted. Even at the risk of falling and breaking a hip—the catastrophe that spells the end for so many old folks—he just had to cop a feel. The wildness in his rheumy eyes, the panting, the crude guttural noises—it was as if there among those ancient sunstruck green hills she had been confronted not by a fellow human being but by some uncontrollable force.

V

There was only one hope she didn't and wouldn't allow herself to hold on to: that if, in almost thirty years, she hadn't found a man, not a single one, who was exclusively significant for her, who had become inevitable to her, someone who was strong and brought her the mystery she had been waiting for, not a single one who was really a man and not an eccentric, a weakling or one of the needy the world was full of—then the man simply didn't exist, and as long as this New Man did not exist, one could only be friendly and kind to one another, for a while. There was nothing more to make of it, and it would be best if women and men kept their distance and had nothing to do with each other until both had found their way out of the tangle and confusion, the discrepancy inherent in all relationships. Perhaps one day something else might come along but only then, and it would be strong and mysterious and have real greatness, something to which each could once again submit.

Perhaps one day. But since these words were written, almost a half century ago, in an autobiographical story by Ingeborg Bachmann, men and women have become only more divided.

The tangle is tighter, the confusion deeper, the discrepancies starker. Red states and blue states. And forget friendly and kind.

A construction worker on-site accidentally backs into a woman on the sidewalk and says, Sorry. She snarls something I don't catch and he responds, I said sorry. She gives him the finger and keeps walking. He calls after her: I said sorry! Without turning around she screams, It's too fucking late to be sorry. Fine, he screams. I take it back. *I'm not fucking sorry.*

What a mess.

An argument with a tableful of women, one of whom tells the story of a woman who, in response to catcalling by a pair of men, dug into her pants, pulled out her tampon, and threw it at them.

I was the only one who thought she should not have done that.

She had a right to defend herself, the others said.

According to Bachmann, fascism is the primary element in the relation between a man and a woman.

Overstated.

Like Angela Carter's assertion that, while behind every great man is a woman dedicated to his greatness, behind every great woman is a man dedicated to bringing her down.

Still.

You write ladies' novels, correct? said the novelist to his female colleague.

Oh what dark neck of the woods have we entered here.

The Bachmann story, "Three Paths to the Lake," appears in her collection *Three Paths to the Lake* (the original German title was *Simultan*), which was published in 1972, a year before she died of burns suffered in a fire. Five stories. Five women, each one suffering from some form of emotional turmoil, each one feeling trapped, isolated, anxious, and confused about her place in patriarchal society, and struggling for a language to express what she's going through.

George Balanchine said, If you put a group of men on the stage, you have a group of men, but if you put a group of women on the stage you have the whole world.

If you put a group of women in a book, you have "women's fiction." To be shunned by almost all male readers and no few female ones as well.

When Bachmann, who from an early age had been renowned for her poetry, began publishing stories, they were dismissed by critics as *Frauengeschichten*, meaning stories about banal and insignificant matters, female concerns of possible interest only to other women. (Bachmann herself first imagined the book as a kind of homage to the women of her native Austria.)

Around the same time that Bachmann's collection was published, in a novel in progress Elizabeth Hardwick wrote: Do you know a happy woman?

The catcalling men turned out to be plainclothes cops. They arrested the woman. I forget how her story ends.

I have learned that there exists a word, *onsra*, in Bodo, a language spoken by the Bodo people in parts of northeastern India, that is used to describe the poignant emotion a person experiences when that person realizes that the love they have been sharing with another is destined not to endure. This word, which has no equivalent in English, has been translated as "to love for the last time." Misleading. Most English-speaking people would probably take "to love for the last time" to mean to have at long last found one's true, enduring love. For example, in a song composed by Carole King called "Love for the Last Time." But when I first learned this translation of *onsra* I thought it meant something else entirely. I thought it meant to have experienced a love so overwhelming, so fierce and deep, that you could never ever ever love again.

I've never liked the genre of women's fiction known as romance, but I am fascinated by stories of women in love, especially when the love is in some way unconventional or especially difficult, hopeless even, or frankly insane.

Women in Strange Love might be the title of a collection of such stories.

Take, for example, the love of the painter Dora Carrington for the writer Lytton Strachey. No matter that she knew he was gay (no matter that he once proposed marriage to Virginia Woolf), or that he was thirteen years older than her. A scandal from the start, theirs became a legendary story. Indeed, it is not for her painting but for her endless, hopeless love of Strachey, how it shaped her life, how it caused her death, that Carrington is known (that kind of woman's story). For seventeen years, she was devoted to him. Not even her marriage to another man could separate them; all three had to live together. But then the man she married was not her but *his* object of desire. Having agreed to the marriage, she wrote a poignant letter to Strachey, lamenting the fate that made it impossible for the two of them to become man and wife. Then all three went to Venice on honeymoon together.

When Strachey died, of stomach cancer, Carrington survived less than two months before shooting herself. *In the stomach*. She was just shy of thirty-nine. Not her first suicide attempt. "There is nothing left for me to do," she had told the Woolfs the day before. "I did everything for Lytton."

She didn't have a gun in the house so she went next door and borrowed one, like a cup of sugar. A rabbit gun. ("Like some small animal left" had been Virginia Woolf's parting impression of her.) The wrong weapon for the job, it seems: meaning a long, slow, painful dying.

D. H. Lawrence, so obsessed with the subject—and so confident in his authority on it—that he wrote a whole novel called *Women in Love*, accused Carrington of hating "real" men. One of the novel's women in love is a caricature: pretty, deceptively innocent-looking Minette *Darrington* is really a deep-down lascivious pervert. And not an artist as Carrington was, but (twist of the knife) an artist's model.

In a short story written many years later, another caricature that Lawrence appears to have based on Carrington is gang-raped and she commits suicide.

VI

I went again to visit my friend. The treatments had failed. The tumors had spread. She was back in the hospital.

I booked the same room where I'd stayed before.

As you'll see, my host texted me, our household has a new member!

A young cat, eyes the color of bourbon, silver gray and sleek as a seal.

I shouldn't have let the grandkids name him, she said. Now he's stuck with Booger.

A rescue cat. They found him trapped in a dumpster, she said. Badly dehydrated and just skin and bones. They didn't think he'd survive. But look at him now!

Nine lives, I said, thinking of my friend. *Badly dehydrated. Just skin and bones.*

She was angry, my friend. She was very angry, she wanted to smash everything in sight, she said. Not at God. She wasn't angry at God, of course not, she didn't believe in God, she said. And certainly not at her doctor, she adored her oncologist, her whole medical team, she said, they had done everything they possibly could for her, and they had been kind. At whom, then? At herself, she said. My first instinct was right, she said. I should have obeyed it. I should never have put myself through all that torture, the vomiting, the diarrhea, the fatigue—*horrific, horrific*—and, in the end—

False hope, she said. I should never have given in to false hope. I can never forgive myself for that, she said. Pause. *Never*: as if that could still mean *a long time*.

And now here we are, she said. And what have I got? Months, maybe. At most a year. But probably not that long.

I'm trying not to panic, she said. I'm trying to keep my head. I don't want to go out kicking and screaming. *Oh no, not me! Not me!* Lashing out in rage, drowning in self-pity. Who wants to die like that? Half-demented with fear.

On the other hand, make no mistake, she said: she was no stoic. She did not want to go through excruciating pain. Pain was something that did terrify her. Pain was the thing that terrified her most. Because you can't be self-possessed if you're in agony, she said. In that kind of pain you can't think straight, you're a desperate animal, you can think of only one thing.

It wasn't as though she were old and frail, she said. All her life she'd taken care of her health, and now she was thinking that all that care, all that regular exercise and healthful eating, would only make things harder. My heart is strong my doctor said, she said. What if that means that my body will keep trying to fight, that I'll have to suffer and suffer up to my last breath.

Like her father, she said. The doctors had given him days but it turned out to be weeks, he had hung on and on, by the time he died he was completely insane. A terrible death, she said. Barbaric. Nobody should have to die like that.

How should a person die, she said. Get her the dummies' guide. Oh but forget books, she didn't want to read anything, she didn't want to do *research*, she said. It was funny, she said, for a while that *is* what I wanted, or thought I wanted, to *educate* myself, the way I did about the cancer itself, to find out as much as I could, and God knows I learned a ton, much of it quite interesting, even fascinating, she said, I sank into it, and reading about it I forgot what I was reading, if that makes any sense, I mean at times I was so absorbed in the material I forgot *why* I was studying it, and isn't that the wonderful thing about reading, how it takes you out of yourself. But all that's changed, she said. I have no desire to read about dying, or death, what the great minds, what the philosophers had to say about it, you could tell me that the smartest person in the world had just written the most brilliant book on the subject and I wouldn't touch it. I don't care. Just as I have no desire to write about what I'm going through. I don't want to spend my last days in the same struggle, the struggle to find the right words—curse of my life, when I think about it. Which surprised me, she said, because at first I thought *of course* I should write about it, and I would write about it, my last book about last things, or *the* thing, *the distinguished thing*, I should say, she said, quoting Henry James. Wouldn't it be impossible *not* to write about it I thought, my friend said. But very soon I changed my mind. I changed my mind, my friend said again, and I know I won't change it back. The idea of writing about what I'm going through makes me sick, she said. Not that I'm not already sick, literally, sick to death, quite literally, what a thought, she said, laughing. You see, there I go again with the fucking words. But what I mean, she said, is that I've had it. I've done enough languaging. I'm sick of writing, sick of word searching. I've said enough—I've said too much. I wish— Am I making any sense?

I assured her that she was making sense, and that she should keep talking.

I've decided I'll write about it only if I discover something new to say about it, she said. Which won't happen.

A good death, she said. Everyone knows what that means. Free of pain, or at least not convulsing in agony. Going out with poise, with a little dignity. Clean and dry. But how often did that happen? Not often, in fact. And why was that? Why was that too much to ask?

She said, You talk now. I can't bear the sound of my own voice anymore.

As on my last visit, I tried talking about the usual things, books I'd read, movies I'd seen, but kept lapsing into silence, at which she would become agitated and start talking herself again.

Do you know who came to see me yesterday?

She named someone I knew only by reputation but who'd been a good friend of hers since journalism school. He'd been fired from his paper's staff and from his teaching position within hours of being accused of a half-dozen incidents of sexual misconduct, including an affair with a TA.

He was always that way, she said. As the bad joke about Harvey Weinstein goes: came out of the womb groping his mother. A dirty old man when he was still in his twenties. He was one of them: always ogling and drooling and unable to keep his hands to himself. Well, I didn't know what to tell him, my friend said. In the blink of an eye his life is destroyed. He'd even thought about suicide, my friend said this man had confessed to her. Imagine, he sat right there where you're sitting and talked about how he might as well end it all, and then he caught himself and started begging my forgiveness for being such an insensitive prick, and *then*, my friend raised her voice as she said, he started crying. I kept saying it was okay, she said, because I couldn't stand to lie here listening to him crying and apologizing, but Jesus, you know, it was not okay, she said, it was anything but okay, my friend said emphatically to me.

That's the one thing I will not tolerate, she went on. *Do

feel bad for me, but no goddamn sniveling or blubbering in front of me. I won't have it, she said. Now I'm sorry I ever confided in him. But he's such an old friend, you know, and so far I haven't told many people. And in fact that's something I have to start thinking about, isn't it, my friend asked rhetorically: Who should I tell and how should I go about telling them. And, more important, who do I want to see. There's a lot to think about. I've been making a list. I have to say goodbye to people, you know. I have to— Should I give a party? I'm serious! Should I make an announcement on Facebook? I've seen people do that. It makes sense, of course, but it seems so bizarre to me. I'm not sure I could bring myself to do that.

I said she didn't have to figure out everything all in one day. I asked her if she'd thought about how—if she was really sure about not doing any more writing—she wanted to spend her time after she left the hospital. And where. Was there someplace she wanted to go, I asked, aware that travel was at the top of most people's bucket list, a term I had heard her object to vehemently long before her diagnosis: Could they have come up with an uglier term?

She didn't know, she said. She waved a limp hand in the air. It's a paradox that I've noticed, she said. I know I'm dying, but when I lie here thinking, especially at night, often it's as if I had all the time in the world.

That must be eternity, I said without speaking.

The nearness of eternity, she agreed silently.

Sometimes I even catch myself wishing the hours would

move a little faster, that the day would end sooner, she said. Adding: Oddly enough, I am often bored.

How will you ever get through this, I thought.

I really don't know, she thought back.

Wouldn't that be something, she said to me, if dying turned out to be a bore.

Her phone rang: her daughter. Her plane had landed, she would be there soon. Was there anything she could pick up for her mother on the way?

I used the interruption to try to calm my emotions by deep breathing.

Oh look, she said. Outside the hospital window it had begun to snow, and because the sun was just going down the snow was tinted a sunset pink.

Pink snowflakes, she said. Well. I've lived to see that.

He's still a kitten, my host said in a tone suggesting enormous pride in him for this. He can be really rambunctious and mischievous, and he tends to roam at night. Make sure your door is closed tight so he won't bother you.

The same paperback mystery on top of the same pile on the nightstand.

The killer makes friends with a woman he meets in a bar, a young actress who has come to the big city from the Midwest in hopes of becoming a Broadway star. Though she finds him morose and maddeningly secretive, she doesn't in the least suspect his crimes. It is through her that he begins to realize his dream of "getting more culture." She lends him books and takes him to art films and museum shows. Far more important, she turns him on to disco dancing. It is the era of *Saturday Night Fever*. The killer turns out to be a spectacularly good dancer who quickly establishes himself as king of the floor. When the woman encourages him to study dance, he throws himself into it, taking classes six days a week, advancing so quickly that he begins to think seriously about a professional career. Now his whole life is transformed. He has never been so happy. But when severe tendinitis forces him to stop dancing, he is crushed. Bitterly, he reflects that, no matter how big his talent, no matter how hard he works, because he started training too late he will never have a shot at fame.

The killer thinks a lot about John Travolta. It turns out that he and Travolta have many things in common: they share the same birthday, they are exactly the same height and weight, they each come from suburbs near Manhattan, they each won a dance competition doing the twist when they were kids, they each had a father who played football. But their mothers could not have been more different. John's mother, an actress and singer herself, had encouraged him to pursue a career in show business, taking charge of his early training. Now, far worse than the pain in his legs, this question torments the killer: What kind of life might *his* have been had *he* had a mother like John Travolta's?

More and more of the killer's time is consumed in a state

of rage against the star. Travolta's high "sissified" voice singing "Summer Nights" becomes stuck in his head, driving
him to distraction. Give him a way and he would kill John
Travolta.

Instead he kills a fellow dance student, stalking him to
his Brooklyn home after class one night. He also impulsively
strangles a college student after having sex with her in Riv-
erside Park.

The police fail to connect the four homicides thus far
committed by the killer. While they remain stymied in their
separate investigations, he continues to hang out with the
unsuspecting actress (now just beginning to find some big-
city success) and her circle of artistic young friends.

The cat came in on little fog feet. I was not even aware
of him until he jumped onto the bed. His whiskers tickled
as he snuffled my cheek. Earlier he had lain by the fireplace.
Is there anything more hygge than lying close to a loudly
purring cat whose warm fur smells of woodsmoke, watching
him knead the duvet?

I closed the book and turned out the light.

I had a decent home, the cat said, his words muffled by
the purr but still clear. I'm not saying it was the lap of luxury.
But I had food and fresh water every day, and a dry bed, and
at the time I'd never known anything better. I was born in a
cage in a shelter, he said. I never knew how sweet, with the
right human, life could be, especially when the human is a
female of a certain age living without a mate.

I was adopted to be a mouser not a pet, he said, and my first home wasn't a nice house like this, it wasn't even a house, it was a store, a convenience store just off the highway, run by an old guy in a wheelchair with his wife and son.

I did my job, the cat said, I kept the mice away, and in return I had my bed—really just a cardboard box with a ratty old bath towel folded in it—and my bowl was kept full of crunchies, and well, that was it, my life, my whole world. The people weren't bad as people go, but they weren't cat people, either, not by a long shot, the cat said, and after I made the mistake of jumping in the guy's lap one day while he was rolling through the aisles only to find myself flying into the cereal boxes I kept my distance. It's strange how wide the range of human responses to our kind is, the cat said. As precious as human young to some, to others we're not much higher than plants, and to still others filthy varmints with no more rights or feelings than a stick.

There was much coming and going through the long hours that the store was open, said the cat, but I tended to keep to myself in the back, and it was rare for anyone to notice me. And though I noticed everyone myself I hardly bothered to look up past their knees. For the truth is, we are less curious than the saying goes, at least in regards to human strangers, who after all do not differ greatly one from another. In the early days after I arrived I thought about my mother a lot (as it happened, I was the last to be adopted, and so for a few blessed days I'd had her all to myself), I missed her, and oh did I cry for her. But I'm a cat, said the cat, and I quickly adjusted to my new situation.

When I came here, to this house, though, after everything I'd been through—including a second stay at the shelter, where there was no longer any trace of my mother, not even her smell—I might as well have been a newborn again, I felt so helpless, said the cat, so puny and scared. And when this lady took charge of me, with her bowls of warm milk and wet-washcloth baths and piles of soft clean bedding, and the way she hovered as I went about investigating each new room, I remembered what it was like to have a mother, and I knew I had found a second one.

It happened in the middle of the night, but luckily the store was still open, the cat (who had stopped purring) went on. The son was working the counter alone and I was asleep in my box when smoke started pouring up from the basement. We were both out of there in a flash—not that he gave me a thought, but I was at his heels when he raced through the door. I ran across the highway and crouched there, not sure what to do. When the fire trucks came it was too much for me—the sirens made my ears hum after for days—so I ran and ran until I was too tired to run anymore. It was freezing that night, said the cat, and I wasn't used to being outdoors. I lost the feeling in my ears and paws—I was afraid they would always stay that way! I crawled under a porch, where I felt at least safer, if not any warmer. When light came, I made my way back home and saw that it was home no more, just a reeking soggy blackened wreck. The front door had been secured with a lock and chain. There was no sign of my peeps.

I sat there in a daze, the cat said, not knowing what I should do. Cars drove by, a few slowing down so that people could gawk, but no one pulled into the lot or took any notice of me. Being small and gray, said the cat, I'm easy to miss.

Then I saw two bicycles approaching. The riders I knew. Bad kids, double trouble, who often played hooky from school, and who on more than one occasion, when it was just the old man in the store, stole candy bars or chips and mocked his helpless rage before riding away.

How I let them catch me is a shameful story, said the cat. Remember, though, how hungry I was and maybe then you'll understand what I felt when one of them pulled out and pushed toward me a balled-up foil wrapper that, even from a distance, smelled divinely of flesh. In my weakened state, it was a cinch for him to seize me by the scruff. The other took hold of my tail, and after swinging me about, all the while whooping and cackling like fiends, they carried me to the dumpster in back of the store. Once they'd tossed me in and rolled the cover shut they kicked and banged away at the sides until at last they got bored and took off.

There I sat at the bottom of that dark cold damp bin, which was empty but slimy with filth, said the cat. I could not stop shaking. What next? Would the brutes return to finish me off? And if they didn't return, how would I ever get out of there? I began to cry, making my voice as big as possible, said the cat, and very big indeed it sounded to me in that void, but no one heard, no one came, and soon I had no voice left to cry anymore. Still I kept opening and closing my mouth in silent meow, as we cats do when in despair.

I must have slept on and off, said the cat, but the cold and the pangs of hunger and thirst kept me mostly awake. Awake, but not alert. My mind was hardly under my control anymore, I felt myself slipping away, into an ever-deeper dark and cold—then I heard a voice.

Holy shit, a rat.

Looking up, I saw blue sky and a large head silhouetted against it. A second head appeared, and there came a different voice: That ain't no rat, dummy, it's a cat.

Oh wow, said the first head. Let's get it out of there.

Nah, said the other. Looks sick to me. Might have rabies. Let's call the ASPCA, let them handle it.

And so, said the cat, who was purring again, I found myself back at the shelter. And one day, after I'd been nursed back to health, I and about a dozen other cats and dogs were loaded onto a bus and driven to a shopping mall.

Call it beginner's luck: my very first Rescue Me Day and I get adopted. The best thing would've been to be reunited with my mother, which was what I was hoping for. But if that was not to be, the next best thing was this lady. She is my second mother, said the beautiful bourbon-eyed silver-furred cat.

He told many other stories that night—he was a real Scheherazade, that cat—but this was the only one I remembered in the morning.

VII

I went to visit my neighbor, an eighty-six-year-old woman who has been living on her own in one of the ground-floor apartments of our building ever since her husband died twenty years ago. This woman once worked as an administrative assistant in some division of our city government. After she retired she got a job as a cashier in a local drugstore, but she hated having to be on her feet for hours at a time so she quit after just a few months. Aside from some babysitting when she was a girl, these two jobs, administrative assistant and drugstore cashier, are the only jobs this woman has had her entire life. The first time I visited her I shocked her by listing all the jobs I'd had since leaving school, some of which I had to struggle to recall. The only thing that appeared to shock her more was my saying that I'd never been married

and didn't have any children. That this could have been a
choice rather than some kind of curse she would not accept.

She has a son who lives in Albany and who comes to see
her once or twice a month, usually on a Sunday, and always
by himself. He and his wife are divorced. He has several
children and grandchildren, but none of them come to visit
the old woman and since she refuses to travel she never sees
any of them. There is just the son, driving down one or two
Sundays each month from Albany, where he works as an ac-
countant for a legal firm.

It used to happen on these visits that he would take his
mother out. I would meet them on their way to a play or a
movie, or I'd see them through the window of our neighborhood Chinese restaurant. She is under five feet tall with
a hump that forces her chin almost to meet her breastbone.
Frail though she is, this gives her a somewhat robust and
even menacing aspect, like some kind of headbutting animal. She has to screw up her eyes when she addresses anyone
who isn't a small child, in a manner that looks painful. Her
son is a rangy man who, to accommodate her while walking
and talking, has to take baby steps and arch himself sideways
like a willow. From a distance they look less like mother
and son than like father and obese child. But these days I
don't see them walking and talking, because the man can no
longer get his mother to go out. For a while he was able to
coax her at least as far as one of the benches in the building
courtyard. But she couldn't sit still. It bothered her that she

was visible to anyone looking out the windows of the apartments facing the courtyard. It didn't matter that these were her neighbors. For one thing, neighbors or not, just about all of them were strangers to her. Long as she has lived in the building—longer than any other tenant, it turns out—she has no friends here. She had a few friends over the years, but they have since moved away, or, like her husband and just about all the friends she's ever had, these people have died.

This kind of fear—the fear of being seen, or watched, or spied on—has begun to consume the woman more and more. Even worse: her fear of being tricked, or cheated.

Some of it is age, her son said to me. Everyone knows old people can be paranoid. But she's not crazy to think she's being preyed on. Her phone rings all day long, he said (meaning her landline, she's never had a cell phone), and it's just one scammer after the next. Everyone gets these kinds of calls, but after you hit a certain age it's like you become this gigantic target. She gets confused by their fast talk and she gets scared, especially when they address her by name. How do they know her name? How did they get her number? Of course she understands what these people are up to and that she has to be on her guard. But she lives in fear that, one way or another, one of these crooks will get around her. Lately she's been obsessed with a story she heard on the news, about a woman who was so ashamed that she'd let some caller rip off her savings that she killed herself. It seems this poor lady was afraid that when her family found out what a stupid thing she'd done they'd declare her incompetent and take away her freedom.

Now that's my mother's biggest fear, the man said. All I have to do is say the words *assisted living* and she threatens to disown me. And really, for her age, she's doing pretty well on her own.

This conversation—our first—took place a couple of years ago, on a bench in the building courtyard. It's something I never do, sit in the courtyard, but I'd accidentally let something burn in the oven and was waiting for my apartment to air out. He was visiting his mother and had stepped out for a smoke. It was a warm dry summer day, there was deep shade from the courtyard trees, the rose trellis was in bloom, and the air was as sweet as city air can get. I hadn't been near a person smoking in a long time, and rather than being unpleasant the smell filled me with nostalgia. Cars packed with teens, college all-nighters, drugs, rock, cocktails, sex. I wouldn't have minded if he'd blown the smoke right in my face rather than deliberately over his shoulder.

His mother's day was a barrage of interruptions, he said. Congratulations, she just won a sweepstakes. She recently stayed at a certain hotel (as a matter of fact, she has stayed in a hotel exactly once in her life, on her honeymoon, more than six decades ago) and is now eligible to receive a reward. The thank-you gift from an anonymous friend is waiting for her. The special life-saving device she ordered is ready to be shipped. She is eligible for a free trip, a new credit card, a preapproved loan, a personalized wellness package, a free home security system. To protect her bank account, she must verify her personal information. A grandchild needs money to get out of jail; another grandchild has been kidnapped and is being held for ransom.

What about the Do Not Call Registry, I asked, and the man shrugged. He'd registered his mother's number but the volume of calls stayed about the same. When I asked why his mother didn't use caller ID, he smiled. She has caller ID, he said. But it's like she can't resist. The phone rings, Mom's got to answer. She wants to know who it is! Also, it's not rational, but she's damned if she's going to let bad people force her to hide from her own phone. And when it's not a robocall but an actual person, though I've warned her never to talk to them, she sometimes does. She starts interrogating them. How do they know her name? How did they get her number? Or she'll play along for a bit, you know, playing the sweet gaga old lady. Then they ask for her social security number and she says, Sure, honey, got a pen? It's one two three, four five, six seven eight nine. When someone told her they had one of her grandkids, she said, That's okay, I got more, and I never liked that one anyway.

Hearing this, it crossed my mind that the woman, all alone all day in her apartment, might actually enjoy these phone calls, that they might be as much a meager kind of entertainment as a nuisance to her. I was reminded of another neighbor I once had, another elderly widow living alone, who used to knock on my door regularly to complain about the noise—baffling me, because I hadn't been making any noise—until I realized that it was something else. A terrible thing was happening to her. Attention must be paid.

Sometimes she tries to reform them, the man said. I've listened to her do this. She starts lecturing them, asking why would they want to hurt innocent people, why didn't they go out and get themselves an honest job. She's even convinced herself that she's had some success. Last month she told me about a guy who told her he was truly sorry for what he'd done and promised never to do it again.

The man laughed, and I laughed with him. He had finished his cigarette, but instead of going back to his mother he kept sitting there on the bench, talking. It occurred to me that she must wonder what was taking him so long, but he didn't seem concerned. I wasn't entirely surprised when he shook another cigarette from his pack and lit up again.

I do worry about her becoming more vulnerable, he said. The older she gets, the more forgetful she is, and things happen. Her toothbrush ends up in the fridge, she has trouble keeping the grandkids straight. And after all, people a lot younger and sharper than her get scammed every day.

I thought about a friend of mine whose mother is in a nursing home. Every time I visit her, he told me, she says something about how maybe now I'll find a nice girl to settle down with. And every time she says this I say to her, No, Mother, I'm gay, remember? This has been going on for years. Every time my friend sees his mother he has to come out all over again.

It's so depressing, the man in the courtyard went on. Like old people don't have enough bad things happening to them. What a toxic society we live in. And it's not just one or two bad apples. Seems like hordes of people are out there ready to prey on the weakest. I don't get it. How do these crooks feel when they've ruined some poor person's life? How can they enjoy whatever it is they spend that victim's money on? Feasting on someone else's misery—how can these people look in the mirror? What do they tell themselves?

I said I thought these people would say that it was only money, that they weren't really hurting anyone, they weren't really evil like killers or rapists or child molesters. I said probably every one of them could point to a time when they themselves had been victims, when some kind of damage had been done to them—especially when they were too young to defend themselves. And who had cared then? Who had been there to look out for *them*? I said they could probably all name a dozen ways in which they'd been cheated out of something they thought they should have. It was a dog-eat-dog world. It was a jungle out there. It was every man for himself. Deal with it.

Is what I said I thought such people told themselves.

The man gave me a sideways glance. That's deep, he said with just a hint of mockery. You a psychologist?

I told him I was a writer.

Interesting, he murmured, his gaze absently tracing the path of his cigarette smoke.

I thought of the Hitchcock movie about a man known as the Merry Widow Murderer. Uncle Charlie, fulminating against rich old widows—"fat, wheezing animals," who, according to him, had no right to all their money. "What happens to animals when they get too fat and too old?" To him, his victims *deserved* to be slaughtered.

Since his mother had stopped going out, the man had arranged for regular deliveries of groceries and other necessities to her door and for someone from a housekeeping service to come in and clean once a week. Certain things, however, had not been cleaned in a long time. Windows, for example. This I would discover when I began visiting the woman, which would never have happened had I not got into a conversation with her son in the courtyard that day.

After Hurricane Sandy, when our building lost power for several days, he'd been beside himself thinking about her all alone in the cold and dark. At least landlines had been working. But, he said, in the next emergency—and there would always be a next—who knew what might happen. For years he'd been trying to get her to move upstate, but she wouldn't budge.

Mom was always a bit on the stubborn side, he said. But now, forget about it. Be like moving the Rock of Gibraltar.

I should say that this was at a low point in my life, when the balance of things to be unhappy about seemed weightier than things to be grateful for (having heard how helpful to a person's emotional well-being it could be, I'd started keeping a gratitude list). They say one way to lift yourself up when you're down is to do something for somebody else. We weren't entirely strangers to each other, my neighbor and I. I too have lived in the building for many years, and she hasn't always been a recluse. There was a time when, meeting in the lobby or in the mailroom, we'd exchange a few words. I agreed to visit this man's mother now and then and to check on her in case of emergency. I didn't think it was asking much. I'd done the same when I lived in another building, for a neighbor who, though still young, had a disability that kept her mostly housebound. Also, if the truth be told, I was hoping that, though it had yet to be put into action, my good deed might help me get through the rest of the day with more success than I'd had so far in the kitchen, maybe even help me get some work done, a main reason for my current funk being that I hadn't got any work done in some time.

After we'd exchanged contact information and the man had thanked me many times over, he politely assumed an interest in me. What kind of writing did I do? Let him guess: romance.

Just then, from overhead, through the open window of one of the second-floor apartments, came a noise. A cry. A female cry. We sat there, momentarily silenced, as the cry glided into a moan.

The bed must have been right under the window. And,

given how any sound made in that brick canyon was much magnified (the cause of frequent tenant complaint), it might as well have been miked.

Together, without a word, and avoiding each other's gaze, we stood up from the bench and headed for the door leading into the building. I kept slightly ahead of him, trying not to run, as the moans pursued us, without pause, rising, rhythmic, weirdly interrogative: *Is it? Is it? Is it is it is it?* Then, just as we made it to the door: *Stop!* we heard the woman shout. *No! No! Stop!*

Did we say goodbye? All I remember now is the man hanging back while I fled upstairs to my apartment, where I slammed the door behind me and leaned against it, tears in my eyes, heart pounding.

I figured it would be an easy obligation to fulfill. I figured she'd want to talk, as people so often do, especially lonesome people, who often talk volubly even to complete strangers about things that have nothing to do with the listener. I expected she'd probably talk about herself, about her long life, her memories of the past, and I wouldn't have to fake attention, because other people's lives, and specifically their remembrance of things past, are a source of genuine interest to me. I think it's largely true, what I once heard a famous playwright say, that there are no truly stupid human beings, no uninteresting human lives, and that you'd discover this if you were willing to sit and listen to people. But sometimes you had to be willing to sit for a very long time. It always amazes me now to think back to when I was an adolescent, and to remember how little attention my friends and I paid to one another's parents and grandparents. What could they possibly have to say, these ordinary people, most of whom, if they weren't housewives or retirees, went to work every day at jobs we couldn't imagine being the least bit interesting. It was only later that it occurred to me that these were people who'd lived through some of the most dramatic events of the century. They themselves had come of age during periods of upheaval, had endured all types of hardship, had escaped harrowing conditions in foreign countries, or in the Deep South, become homeless during the Depression, fought in world wars, been held captive in prisons, survived death camps. They had been through some of the most extreme things life can throw at a person, like characters in the movies we saw, but although we might have had some vague idea of this, from those movies, say, compared to what kind of clothes or makeup your girlfriends were wearing, it could not provoke the slightest curiosity. My friends and I hung on one another's every word, we were transfixed by the minutiae of our BF's experiences, no matter that they were all but identical to our own. I had a classmate whose father had worked for J. Edgar Hoover, another whose mother was an ER nurse. These people had *stories*—the same kind of stories that had us rapt in front of the TV night after night. But we wouldn't have dreamed of engaging them in conversation, and if they'd ever started talking openly about themselves we would have died.

Later still, though, I realized that, even among themselves, with other grown-ups, including those closest to them, most of these people were not at all eager to talk about the past, especially the traumatic parts. Who wanted to remember? Who wanted to hear? Only those who are writers, it seems, get to say what happened.

Untold is a good word. Meaning, of course, not recounted or narrated. But also, too much or too many to say. The untold story of his youth. Untold suffering.

The air in the homes of old people, have you noticed, is always stale. Even when the windows were open I felt stifled. Usually when I dropped by, in the afternoon, she had the blinds closed and the only light in the room came from the television, which seemed to be always on. I didn't want her to go through any trouble so I always came with coffee and muffins that I'd bought at the corner coffee bar. This she clearly appreciated, and I was grateful for the way it gave some structure to these visits, something for us to do, something to share, and, once the coffee and muffins were finished, it was not too awkward to use this as a sign that it was time for me to go.

She was a big complainer. Mostly she complained about our building: the garbage piling up in the basement, the super

who took too long to fix things and whose English she had
so much trouble understanding, the high-heeled clacking of
her neighbor upstairs ("in her Jimmy Choo-choos"), children
throwing balls in the courtyard. She was particularly irritated
that the smell from the litter box of someone's cat occasionally
drifted through the vents into her own bathroom. (This happened once when I was there; in fact it was the smell of someone smoking weed, but I didn't say this.) She batted away
questions about her early life. She didn't like to remember being young, she said. It just made her feel old. About my own
life she had no curiosity. I was single, I was childless: *What*
life? Once she'd finished complaining about the building she
moved on to the world at large, her feelings about which could
be summed up in four words: *hell in a handbasket.*

It was summer again and I went away, I had some traveling to do, and when I returned six weeks later I learned that
while I was gone she had been briefly hospitalized for what
her son described only as a coronary event. She didn't seem to
me much changed at first: same old litany, more or less, but
the countdown to the presidential election had begun, and
she was becoming increasingly agitated. Was it really possible
that Americans would elect to the highest office in the land,
to the most powerful position on earth, a person so manifestly
unfit, so brazenly immoral and corrupt, a person who lied
with every breath and was a complete incompetent to boot?

Never had my neighbor's faith in humanity been so
shaken.

That woman is as crooked as a barrel of fishhooks, she said. Worse even than the great Obamination. The woman had blood on her hands, she was a treasonous traitor, she deserved to be shot, my neighbor said. How could she ever have got this far? Of course it was some kind of conspiracy.

I myself have never had that much interest in politics, her son said to me. Right now I don't like what I'm seeing on either side, so I may just sit this one out. But the thing is, Mom was never like this before. I mean, she never got worked up over an election, and when I was growing up she and Dad usually voted Democrat. And Mom even used to be a feminist. I don't mean in any active political way, but I remember her reading that book (*The Feminist Mystic*, he called it), and I remember her talking about women's liberation and what a great thing it was and what a bad thing it was that more women weren't in office.

Not to sound crazy myself, he said, but when I listen to her now it's like while she was in the hospital someone planted a chip in her brain. She thinks Christians are under attack, she thinks Hillary Clinton is some kind of—I don't really know what, but I've heard her say Hillary Clinton answers to Satan. But the thing is, Mom's not religious, she never has been, and I never knew her to believe in Satan. So where did this come from? And how is it that, no matter what it's about, if it's between what Sean Hannity says or what her own son says, she trusts Hannity.

I'm sorry, he said, I know you've been getting an earful, but I think after the election she'll calm down.

But after the election she did not calm down. She remained just as paranoid, just as enraged at the enemies of Christianity and of real, patriotic Americans. She took it ill when I happened to remark that Sean Hannity reminded me of Lou Costello, as if I'd said it to slander him.

But in fact, one of the strangest things about her behavior was that she didn't really care what I said. She never paused during one of her rants to ask whether I agreed or disagreed with her, never asked what my own views of the two candidates were, and when I volunteered such information she received it with a shrug, she never made the least effort to convert me. I could watch Fox News for myself if I wanted the truth, and if I didn't, to hell with me.

For the most part, though, it was as if I weren't even there. Never have I felt more superfluous. The coffee and muffins might as well have been left there by elves. I began to wonder what my visits could really have meant to her. I supposed I functioned successfully as some kind of ear, but there didn't seem to be any real human connection. I had started visiting her out of the desire to do a good thing, something that would benefit another person—two persons, if you counted her son. But could it still be called good if I'd begun to hate every minute of it, to regret that I'd ever agreed to it in the first place, that I'd ever laid eyes on either of them, that the woman had ever been born? Wasn't this really rather what you'd call a sick situation? Aside from the anxiety that built up for days before I could bring myself to ring her bell again, there were moments when I found myself actually afraid of her, when her voice was raised in anger and she glowered from her humpbacked position out of bloodshot rolled-back eyes and I feared she really was going to headbutt me across the coffee table.

On the other hand, I didn't know how to get out of these visits now, what I would tell her son (the truth, or some excuse?), or the woman herself (but would she even care?), and I felt increasingly stuck in a position that seemed both perverse and ridiculous.

It's so sad was one of the last things her son ever said to me. If she never watched TV, he said, I know she wouldn't be this way. And it makes me so mad. She could be spending her last years in relative comfort and peace, grateful for what she has. Instead she's in a constant state of bitterness and resentment toward all the enemies she's been scared into thinking are out to get her. It's so sad, what happens to old people. I keep telling myself it's not her fault, same thing could happen to me. But I know I'd rather die before my time than have it ever happen to me.

At the very end of his very long life, a college professor of mine who'd devoted his youth to the cause for human rights was down to a vocabulary of just a few (shrieked) words, one of which was *faggot* and the other the N-word.

I went away again, and this time while I was gone it was the man who suffered a coronary. This I learned from another neighbor after my return. Not long after the funeral, he told me, some relatives had come and taken the man's mother away. Where to, he didn't know. Most of her belongings were still in the apartment, though, and it was another month before the same relatives came and removed them. Soon after that a young couple moved in. I've never spoken to either of them, but I noticed recently that they are expecting a baby.

It shouldn't have been too hard to find out my old neighbor's new address, and that, I told myself, was precisely what I should do, and I should send her a note of condolence. But the relief I felt at discovering her gone was so great that I felt there was less shame in my keeping silent.

What are you going through? When Simone Weil said that being able to ask this question was what love of one's neighbor truly meant, she was writing in her native French. And in French the great question sounds quite different: *Quel est ton tourment?*

VIII

My friend begins the most important conversation of our lives by asking if I've heard that Einstein's private writings include several examples of racist stereotyping and that he was also an abusive husband. I tell her that I have and she says, So I guess there goes the theory of relativity.

I gamely chuckle and ask how she's feeling. She looks bad to me, haggard and jaundiced, though probably not worse than the last time I saw her. New: a tremor in her hands, and from time to time just talking leaves her short of breath.

I did a very stupid thing, she says.

You're allowed, I say—then immediately worry that she'll think I meant *because you're dying.*

She had agreed to do a radio podcast in which she would respond to questions about what it was like to be terminally ill. A social worker at the hospital had somehow got her to do it, she says, and she should have known it was a mistake. It had gone badly, she says, *off the rails*, as she put it, partly because she was in pain, and she was also light-headed from not eating, she said, she hadn't been able to keep anything down that day, and she should have known how irritating the questions would be. Or, even if they weren't truly irritating, how likely she'd be to find them so.

Too late to do anything about it now, she says glumly.

So what, who cares? I say—and again I wish I could unsay it, fearing that she'll hear *you're dying*.

You're right, she says. I shouldn't give a fuck. But when your time is short and you spend any of it badly—you waste any of it doing something stupid—well it sucks. Not to mention not wanting one of your last impressions this side of paradise to be falling flat on your face.

I'm sure it wasn't as bad as you think, I say—sincerely: I have never known her to give a bad impression in public.

I have forgotten to set the scene. We are at a bar. Before coming to visit a few days ago, she had specifically asked if we could meet here, at this bar where we used to hang out often, sometimes every night of the week, when we were roommates (along with one other woman with whom we've both long since lost touch) in a nearby tenement. My friend has been staying at a hotel, insisting that she prefers a hotel room to being anyone's houseguest, though she doesn't particularly like hotels she has always abhorred being a houseguest, and even though she has several close friends who live here and the main purpose of this trip is to spend time with them, and, if she isn't feeling too weak—*and if my heart can stand it*, she said—to visit a few places that had special meaning for her, from the days when she lived here too. Our meeting at the bar, our having drinks together, will be the only time we see each other before she goes back home.

It used to be a dive, aswarm with barflies, serving cheap drinks, the only food a few prepackaged bar snacks. There was a pool table and a vintage Wurlitzer and of course you could smoke, which pretty much everyone, including the two of us, did. Now gentrified along with the neighborhood, it has an oversized binder of overpriced wines, a stale-looking tapas buffet where the pool table once stood, and a loud, jazzy playlist. There is a TV screen above either end of the bar, each on mute and tuned to a different station, one news, one sports.

The only business on the block to have survived all these years—and doing quite well, from the size of the crowd—if with every ounce of character erased. This we deplore; this we mourn. But it is still holy ground of our youth, from where how many times did we stumble home, propping each other up, more than once stopping so one or the other could vomit between parked cars. You know she's your girlfriend when she holds the hair out of your face while you puke. We'll drink to that.

I will not go out in mortifying anguish.

I am not surprised to hear her say this. First of all, it's something she has said before. I had an idea that I understood, that I had accepted that probably this was how it would be. But a whole other feeling floods me now when she reveals that she is in possession of a euthanasia drug.

I don't know what to say.

I'm hoping you'll say yes.

Yes—to what?

To my asking for your help.

My hel—? My larynx spasms, causing me to gulp cartoonishly. And her to smile.

I'm not talking about help dying, she says. I know what to do. It's not complicated.

What *is* complicated is what should happen between now and then.

First of all, she says, I can't say for sure how much time that will be.

Understood that she wants to suffer as little as possible.

But I also want things to be as calm as possible, she says. I want everything to be in good order.

She wants to go somewhere, she says. I don't mean travel. Travel would be a distraction. That's not what I'm looking for. And if I did go back to some place that I loved or where I was very happy (Greece, for example, where she'd had the romance of her life, or Buenos Aires, where she'd had her best-ever vacation)—well, you know what they say. Never return to a place where you were really happy, and in fact that's a mistake I've already made once in my life, and then all my beautiful memories of the first time were tainted.

·I could have told her that I've made that mistake too. More than once.

Not that she'd be against taking some little trip, she says. But what I really want is to find some quiet place, it doesn't have to be far away—in fact it shouldn't be too far—and it doesn't have to be anything particularly special, just somewhere I can be peaceful and do the last things that need to be done. And think my last thoughts, she adds as her breath runs out. Whatever they might be.

I relax my grip on my glass. So all she's asking is for me to help her find this ideal place. I ask her whether she's sure about wanting to be in a strange place rather than home.

I think it will make it easier, she says. So long as it's a comfortable, safe, attractive place. I've done a lot of my best work—my best thinking—away from home, on visiting fellowships, for example, on meditation retreats, even in hotels. I think it will be easier to prepare—to focus on letting go—if I'm someplace where I won't be surrounded by intimate, familiar things, all those reminders of attachments, and so on.

Of course I could be wrong, she says, and this could all turn out to be some kind of fantasy. But I've thought a lot about it, and it feels right to me. Am I making any sense?

I think so, I say. And you need my help finding a place, or helping you get settled in?

No, she says. I can do that myself. I've already started looking.

She lays one palm flat on the table and presses her other hand on top of it to quell—or hide—the tremor.

What I need is someone to be there with me, she says. I'll want some solitude, of course, it's what I'm used to, after all, what I've always craved—dying hasn't changed that. But I can't be completely alone. I mean, this is a new adventure— who can say what it will really be like. What if something goes wrong? What if *everything* goes wrong? I need to know there's someone in the next room.

Epic struggle to keep my composure, to choose my words.

I agree, I say. You shouldn't be alone.

But, I ask her after a pause, wouldn't it be more comforting to have someone there who was closer to her? Someone from her family? Back in the days when we'd haunted this bar we might have been joined at the hip, but although we'd always stayed in touch she and I had gone our very separate ways over these many long years, and what she appears to be asking is baffling to me. Plus I'm still trying to absorb the shock of her revelation about the drug.

Someone from my family, she repeats flatly. Well, that would be my daughter—I don't have any other close family members—and I couldn't possibly ask her, it wouldn't be right. It's not just that she and I are anything but comfortable with each other. But precisely because of that—because our relationship has always been so troubled—to be blunt, it would be too much of a mindfuck. She might agree, out of a sense of duty. But given the hostility she's always had toward me, I don't know how she'd ever cope with her feelings. No, I don't see how I can justify putting her in such a position. And there's the added complication of her being the main beneficiary of my will.

Our waiter approaches to ask whether we'd like another round, ignoring that my friend's glass is still full. (This is just for show, she'd said earlier, waving a hand over her gin and tonic. I can't drink on these meds. You'll have to drink for both of us.) My own glass was drained some time ago and no sooner is the waiter gone than I reach for hers. For a moment she watches me with an amused expression, then says, I know your feelings won't be hurt when I say that you weren't my first choice.

Her two closest friends have said no. They could never be a part of any kind of assisted dying, they told her, not even indirectly. Even though they understood why she had come to such a decision and how much they, too, did not want her to suffer, they could never stand by while she took her own life, they would try to stop her. No, they said. No. No.

This is how it is with people, she tells me now. No matter what, they want you to keep fighting. This is how we've been taught to see cancer: a fight between patient and disease.

Which is to say between good and evil. There's a right way
and a wrong way to act. A strong way and a weak way. The
warrior's way and the quitter's way. If you survive you're a
hero. If you lose, well, maybe you didn't fight hard enough.
You wouldn't believe all the stories I get about this or that
person who refused to accept the death sentence they got
from those nasty stupid doctors and was rewarded with
many, many more years of life. People don't want to hear *terminal*, she says. They don't want to hear *incurable*, or *inoperable*. They call that defeatist talk. They say insane things like
As long as you stay alive there's a chance. And *Medical miracles happen every day*—as if they'd been keeping track. They
say, If you just hang in there, who knows, they might find
a cure. I never knew that so many smart, educated people
were under the illusion that a cure for cancer is just around
the corner.

Not that I think they all really believe what they're saying, she goes on, but they obviously believe it's what they
should say. Quite a few people tried to convince me not to
stop working. You have to make every effort, she says those
people said to her, you have to keep working. You have to
carry on was what they meant, she says. Carry on as if all
were well and maybe then all *will* be well. Like, fake it till
you make it, says my friend, laughing herself out of breath.
Chemo might give you acne and a mouth full of sores, but
you must keep putting on lipstick.

The only way people seem able to deal with this disease, she says, is to make it a hero narrative. Survivors are heroes, unless they're kids, in which case they're superheroes, and even doctors, who are just doing their goddamn job, are said to be taking *heroic measures*. But why should cancer be some kind of test of a person's mettle? I can't tell you how much trouble I've had with that, she says. There's almost nothing anyone's said to me that hasn't been some banality or cliché. I quit social media because I had to get away from all the noise. Some of the worst comes from the cancer support community—think of your cancer as a gift, an opportunity for spiritual growth, for developing resources you never knew you had, think of cancer as a step in the journey to becoming your best self. I mean, seriously. Who wants to die listening to that crap.

An exaggerated shuddering motion as she catches her breath.

There comes a point, she goes on, when, if it's really what you want to hear, your doctor will give it to you straight. Incurable. Inoperable. Terminal. Personally, she says, though no one ever uses it I prefer the word *fatal*. *Fatal* is a good word. *Terminal* makes me think of bus stations, which makes me think of exhaust fumes and creepy men prowling for runaways. But back to what I was saying: I've done my research. I know what I'm in for if I let nature run its course. Palliative care can only do so much. I don't see the point of lingering in hospice, getting more and more helpless until I can't do anything for myself anymore. People ought to be able to understand that this is *my* way of fighting, she says. Cancer can't get me if I get me first. And what's the sense in waiting, she says, when I'm ready to go. What I need now is someone who understands all this and who'll promise to stand by me and not go and do something idiotic like flush the pills down the toilet while I'm asleep.

It occurred to me, she says, that maybe I should look for someone who's not so close to me right now, someone I trust but who I'm not used to seeing all the time and who's not used to seeing me. There was another old friend who came to mind who happens also to be a doctor and who in many ways would've been ideal. But she can't just leave her practice. That's been another consideration, my friend says: people have jobs.

Including me. But, as my friend is quick to mention, it's summertime. School is out.

I say, for something *to* say, that I wish we weren't in a public place.

Ah, but that was deliberate, she says. I thought it would keep us from getting—overemotional. But also, I couldn't resist when I thought of that time you and I sat right here in this bar and discussed this very subject.

I have no idea what she's talking about.

Introduction to Ethics. You don't remember? The professor

divided the class into pairs, and each pair had to debate a given
ethical question. Ours was on the right to die. Sanctity of life
versus quality of life. We worked on it together over a couple
of pitchers of beer. Remember? You argued that a person had
a right to take their own life under any circumstances, not
just in terminal cases. It was the individual's business and nobody else's, least of all the state's. I remember that this made
me nervous, she says, because back then you were depressed
a lot and you could also be very impulsive, and hearing you
argue so passionately for suicide freaked me out.

I am so stunned that I almost jump to my feet. Not that
I haven't seen it before: a person tells a story from the past
that they vividly recall when in fact the story is completely
invented. And not that I think my friend is lying; on the
contrary, I know that she has just spoken in all innocence.
I know that what's happened is this: her imagination has
supplied her with a memory to help make a particular way
of thinking about a traumatic situation more coherent. It's
perfectly likely that she and I once discussed the question
of a person's right to die. It's more than likely that I'd taken
the position that she said I had. Maybe I really was the
chronically depressed and impulsive young woman that she
recalled. But she and I had never worked together in this
bar or anywhere else on any such course assignment. I have
never taken Introduction to Ethics.

All of which, however, I leave unsaid. Indeed, I don't say
anything about anything. I am not feeling well. Two drinks

guzzled in a row. But it's not just the alcohol that's making the room spin.

I know what you're thinking, she says. You're thinking, I can't believe we're having this conversation! It's a big thing I'm asking, I know. A huge responsibility. You don't have to give me an answer now. Unless, of course, you can?

I shake my head. Seeing how hesitant I am, she says, Oh, come on. Where's your sense of adventure?

To which I can only shake my head again.

All right then, she says. I'll be going home tomorrow. I'll call you when I get there.

As we are walking out of the bar I stop and say I'd better go to the restroom.

Are you going to be sick? she asks.

Maybe, I say over my shoulder.

Do you want me to hold your hair?

It's down to two places, she said. One was a summer house on an island off the southern Atlantic coast. It belonged to the family of a cousin of hers who wasn't planning to use it till later in the season. She and this cousin had never known each other well, but when he first heard about her illness he was kind enough to offer it for a little getaway. She'd been there once, many years ago, for a wedding, and she remembered how beautiful the house and the beach were, but even this early in the season the island was likely to be full of tourists, she said, and it was not so easy to get to, and besides, she said, I don't want to spend the last days of my life in a red state.

So she was leaning toward the other place, the New England home of a retired couple, former college professors who now spent most of their time traveling and used Airbnb to book short-term renters whenever possible to help finance their trips.

We could have it for a month, she told me over the phone. Not that I think I'll need that much time.

Would I ever get used to this kind of talk? Even as I wondered what to do about my mail—let it pile up, have the post office forward it or hold it for me—I found it unthinkable to ask how long I should plan to be gone.

It's not like I've picked a date, she said. Though, as I say, I am ready to go. You could even say I'm *impatient* to go, which comes partly from my having already given so much thought to dying but also from having reached the limits of what I think I can bear. But I don't know what my body will do.

Though she'd been feeling much better since she went off chemo, her symptoms could change from day to day, and the meds she was taking to suppress them had some side effects too.

In any case, I want things to happen naturally, she said. I feel like I'll know when it's time.

But you—well, you won't know, she said. Obviously I won't be making a big announcement.

Like the coming of the Lord, she said jokingly: *You will not know the day or hour.*

She had decided not to tell anyone about our plans. I've come this far, I don't want to risk some stupid intervention, she said, or even a tiny disruption. I want peace.

No one was to know where we were.

And, for your own protection, she told me, you need to play dumb: I never told you what I was going to do, you weren't even aware that I had the drug.

I had, in fact, already told one other person everything, but I did not say this.

A photo of the colonial-style house had brought to mind the house where she'd grown up. They were both built in the 1880s, she said, though this one's smaller. She told me how heartbroken she'd been about selling her childhood home. But after her parents died, neither she nor her daughter saw themselves ever living in such a big house in what had by then unfortunately become an overdeveloped suburb. Among other things that she liked about the retirees' house, she said, was that it had been renovated with the needs of the aging in mind. There was a large bedroom on the ground floor with its own bathroom in which grab bars and a built-in shower seat had been installed. Given how frail she was now and how, some days, she had trouble walking, this was a lucky thing, she said. Also, the original master bedroom, on the second floor, was at the opposite end of the house. So we'll each have our privacy, she said. (What

I would do with all that privacy was, for me, a very big and daunting question.)

The neighboring houses were spaced well apart and one side of the property bordered a nature preserve.

I don't know the town well, but I have passed through it, she said. I've always been fond of New England coastal towns. And I like that there are supposed to be some good restaurants, now that I've started being able to enjoy food again.

In fact, she didn't really need to give it any more thought. This place looks perfect, she said.

Such excitement in her voice—anyone would have thought we were planning a vacation.

I'm sending you photos, she said, and shortly after we hung up they arrived. Half a dozen shots of the house, inside and out. One of the yard at autumn's red-and-gold peak, another in pristine snow. I stared at them in a kind of stupor. I did not care what house, what town we were in. How much *she* cared was almost unbearably poignant to me.

She had just a few more things to do at home, she said. A few more drawers to empty, a bit more paperwork, some people to see one last time.

A week had passed since we met in the bar.

Start packing, she texted.

I was mechanically layering clothes in a suitcase when she texted again: Thank you for doing this.

When I had told her the answer was yes, that I would do whatever she needed me to do to help her die, her relief had been so great that she began sobbing.

Seconds later, she texted again: I promise to make it as much fun as possible.

PART TWO

Death is not an artist.

—Jules Renard

The house was as advertised. Gracious, clean, and orderly, with a few special welcome touches: flowers in the bedrooms, the kitchen stocked with coffee and tea, juice, yogurt, bread, and other basics. Extra pillows, extra blankets, wood for the fireplace—everything appeared to have been thought of by the hosts (awarded by Airbnb the status of Superhosts), who before leaving for Europe had sent us directions to the house and the code to unlock the front door.

There were no photographs, we noticed right away—we assumed they'd been put into storage with other private belongings and documents—but the living room was dominated by a painting of a woman who we figured must represent the lady of the house in her youth. A life-size oil that brought to mind John Singer Sargent's portrait of Madame X. In fact, the painting might have been just that: an imitation of Sargent. A white swan of a woman with an impossibly long neck in a simple black décolleté dress that exposed the top halves of her—to mix bird metaphors—ostrich-egg-like breasts. One hand rests on the back of a chair, and in the other she is holding a lily. A coy mix of the erotic and the austere.

If it really is her, my friend said, I don't see how she can stand it. How can her *husband* stand it. I mean, living every day with this glaring reminder of how young and hot she used to be.

I shrugged. You know how it is when you live with something every day, I said. They probably don't even notice it anymore.

True. But I can imagine how every time someone sees it for the first time they say, Oh, is that you? You know how people always say that to you when they see a flattering old photo: Is that *you*? And you wince, because they've just let you know how much you don't look like that anymore, it might as well be somebody else. It's humiliating. It shouldn't be, but it really is humiliating.

I agreed that it was humiliating. On the other hand, I said, lots of people display their wedding photos from many years ago.

Well, it's one thing to display a photo of yourself as a bride, but *this* . . .

Whatever, she said. It's an eyesore. It throws the whole room off.

We could drape a sheet over it.

My friend laughed. Oh God, no. That would be even more unsettling.

There were other paintings throughout the house, mostly landscapes or seascapes. In the dining room: a large framed black-and-white photograph of the house itself, dated 1930.

I was relieved that, the eyesore aside, the house matched my friend's expectations.

It reminds me even more of where I grew up, she said. My parents could have had the same decorator. Not that they'd ever in a million years have handed the keys over to a series of total strangers. How much people have changed.

I liked the house too. The arrangement of well-made furniture against just enough polished bareness. Some handsome ceramics but few other household ornaments. That balance of comfort and simplicity that I have heard called Shaker luxe.

It was the middle of the afternoon. Our drive had been delayed by several heavy downpours, but, cheeringly enough, the sun broke through at the very instant the house came into view. On the way, we'd eaten the avocado and tomato sandwiches I'd prepared for us that morning. Now all we wanted was coffee. When we'd made a pot we each took a mug to our room. We had decided that after unpacking we'd go for a quick tour of the town followed by an early dinner.

There was a fish restaurant that had been extolled on some foodie website my friend had been browsing. I couldn't help feeling, though, that this was for my sake. Though her ability to taste—and keep down—food was much better than it had been during her various bouts of chemo, her appetite was anything but robust. I pretended not to notice that it had taken her almost an hour to finish her avocado and tomato sandwich.

I had lurched through the past week like a drunk, all my senses curiously muffled, but now I could not have been more sharply aware of everything: the hot light pouring through the bedroom windows, the smell and taste of the coffee, the cloud-like pillows against the bed's sky-blue duvet, the grain of the blond-wood floor where a brilliantly colored kilim rug lay vibrating like a piece of op art. The closet and the bureau drawers smelled of lavender. (Downstairs I'd noticed a different scent: a fruity astringent tang, like a citrus cocktail.)

Under other circumstances, this would have been a fine place to work. But I doubted whether I'd have the concentration even to browse the news. What I'd imagined myself doing instead was streaming movies and binge-watching episodes of all the great TV series I'd missed in recent years and thought I'd never catch up on. I also took it for granted that I'd be responsible for whatever cooking or cleaning or errands needed doing, and which I knew I'd be more than happy to do, concerned only that there wouldn't be enough such work to keep me busy.

Best try not to anticipate too much was the advice I'd given myself. Though my friend seemed utterly sure of her decision—not once so far had I seen her waver—at the back of my mind was the suspicion that things were not going to happen as planned. Just because we were here now didn't mean she'd definitely take the drug. She'd come here to think, after all, and thinking might lead to changing her mind. Maybe she'd decide to put off taking it for a while longer. (Most dying patients in possession of a lethal dose of medication, I happened to know, never did take it.) In any case, it was far easier for me to imagine that, after a week or so, we'd be leaving this house together than that I'd be leaving it alone.

I was fully aware, and troubled by my awareness, that a big part of me, while agreeing to help my friend, had not truly accepted—was in fact apparently powerfully resisting—the reason we were here. Why *I* was here.

A dozen times since agreeing to be with her till the end I had quailed, had told myself I'd made a serious mistake, it was impossible, in fact I couldn't do it. Then I would think how equally impossible it was for me to back out. I thought that I should at least tell her about these qualms, to which she had responded that she was going to do it anyway.

You want me to do it alone? Because I'll tell you, I don't have the time or energy to go down the list of everyone I know. I want peace.

I want peace was something she'd started saying a lot.

Where's your sense of adventure? As if that could have per-
suaded me! In fact, the real reason I had agreed to help my
friend was that I knew that, in her place, I would have hoped
to be able to do exactly what she now wanted to do. And I
would have needed someone to help me. (In coming days,
there would be moments when I would not be able to escape the feeling that this was all a kind of rehearsal, that my
friend was *showing me the way.*)

It was while I was unpacking that it occurred to me that
I should keep a journal. It still felt all wrong to me that my
friend's daughter, her only family, was not involved in what
was happening, had not even been informed about it. I understood my friend's thinking in this regard and could see
how she might be right, but it saddened me, and it made me
feel guilty, as of a kind of betrayal. Not that it would have
done for me to go behind her back and get in touch with her
daughter, but at the very least I wanted to have a record to
pass on. I thought, when the time came, those who'd been
close to my friend would want to know what she was like,
what she had said and thought and felt, toward the end. It
would be important, then, to be as detailed and as accurate as
possible, and certainly memory alone could not be trusted. I
thought also that sitting down to write about each day would
help—as keeping a journal of other experiences, including
some very difficult ones, though perhaps none as singular as
this, had helped me to keep my bearings.

An adventure? If so, it was two different adventures we

were on, hers completely different from mine, and to whatever extent we might be sharing the days to come, each of us would be very much by herself.

Someone has said, When you are born into this world there are at least two of you, but going out you are on your own. Death happens to every one of us, yet it remains the most solitary of human experiences, one that separates rather than unites us.

Othered. Who is more so than the dying?

I should make a list, I thought. I'd made a lot of lists since all this began, endless to-do lists—as Scott Fitzgerald once pointed out people are wont to do when they're on the verge of a crack-up. My way was to make a list then proceed to ignore it; instead of ever even looking at it again, I'd sit down and make a new one.

But groceries—didn't we need groceries? Of course we did. Tomorrow I'd go grocery shopping, and for that I should have a list.

When I'd finished unpacking, when I'd sat down at the desk in a wedge of sunlight and written out my grocery list, I was pleased to take my measure and conclude that I was in a reasonable state of calm. In one corner of the room stood a beautiful antique cheval looking glass. *I will get through this*, I assured it, and—smiling at the serendipitous wordplay—I went downstairs.

Where my calm was shattered by the sight of my friend slumped at the kitchen table in tears.

My first thought was that she had changed her mind. Now that we'd arrived she'd realized that she didn't want to be here after all. For this, as I've said, I was prepared.

You won't believe what I did, she wailed.

My whole body blazed into panic. Had she, in a wild impulsive moment, taken the drug just this minute? But she couldn't have. She wouldn't have.

I forgot them!

What?

The pills, of course. What else. I keep them hidden, you know, in my bedroom, in the back of a drawer, and when I was packing I forgot to take them out.

I nearly staggered from relief.

We have to go back, she said.

Of course! We can go first thing tomorrow.

Not tomorrow. *Now.*

I didn't think she could be serious.

I have to be sure I didn't lose them or misplace them, she said, her voice rising. I have to know they're there. I have to know that they haven't been stolen or something. That they haven't somehow vanished into thin air. *That I didn't just dream them up in the first place.*

She was clutching her hair in her fists. I was afraid she'd start tearing it out, like a madwoman.

We have to go, and we have to go *now.*

Later, with the pills safe in their new hiding place in her room, and the two of us at the end of our meal at the exquisite fish restaurant, where we were dining for the second night in a row, I quietly suggested that maybe her leaving the pills behind meant that she was conflicted about taking them. After all, she had remembered to bring all her other medications—and there were so many of them!

Fuck you, I am not conflicted. And I told you never to say that to me.

I don't remember you telling me that.

Well, maybe not in so many words. Anyway, you're wrong. I know exactly what it was that made me forget. Chemo brain.

I knew what chemo brain was, but when I didn't say anything she went on to explain.

Memory lapses, attention problems, spacing out, trouble processing information. It can happen even after the treatments stop. It can even get worse after the treatments stop. Cognitive dysfunction. It can last for years, in some cases for the rest of a person's life. I could give you a ton of examples, she said.

Once, mailing a package, she addressed it to herself instead of the person she meant to send it to. She went to buy shoes, and even though she tried them on she ended up buying the wrong size. Then she did the same thing buying pants. She kept losing things: keys, wallet, phone.

Everything I wrote had to be proofread a hundred times, she said, and each time I found at least one error I'd missed before. I couldn't trust my judgment about anything anymore.

Twenty percent to the driver, I'd be thinking. Then in my confusion I'd make it twenty *dollars*.

I wanted to ask her then how she could trust the momentous decision that had brought us here. How did she know that wasn't chemo brain too?

II

The wonder of certain coincidences.

Checking the time, I tap my phone, which is sitting on top of a book on my desk, which happens to be Ben Lerner's novel *10:04*, and see that the time is 10:04.

Reading about a new movie while holding the cat against my shoulder. At the instant I come to the word *vampire*, the cat, which has never bitten me before, sinks its teeth in my neck.

On Columbus Day I see that my checking account balance is exactly $1,492.

A violent altercation between two men reported in the news. A white man and a black man. The white man's surname is Black, the black man's is White.

And here, in this house, on a bookshelf in the living room: *A psychological thriller in the tradition of Highsmith and Simenon, set in the seamy noirish world of seventies New York.*

Not so wondrous. Lots of people have the same books. What *is* wondrous is that the book is dog-eared at the very page—the beginning of a new chapter—where, last time, I left off.

The killer is a heavy drinker. His hip new friends share the popular belief that smoking pot is a cure for alcoholism, but he is wary of drugs. One day they get him to eat a brownie without revealing that it contains hash. After this he takes greedily to cannabis but without giving up alcohol, becoming instead a chronic user of both. As his conduct grows increasingly disturbing, the actress begins to regret having ever befriended him—especially after he seduces her best friend, who falls madly in love with him only to find herself abused and abandoned. But it's the killer's addictions that are his undoing. Worsening paranoia and lack of self-control lead to erratic behavior that in turn leads to a vague suspicion that he knew the woman found strangled in the park. After she is raped by the killer, the actress takes her suspicions to the police. Later, she calls on all her acting skills to set the killer up, manipulating him into a confession that is recorded on equipment that police have installed in her apartment. At the same time she narrowly escapes being murdered herself.

During his trial, the killer, aware of all the attention his case has drawn, imagines that a book about him will be written—a best-selling book that will then be made into a major motion picture. It occurs to him that whoever plays him in the movie will have to be not just a good actor but also a great dancer. That, of course, would be John Travolta. And that is how we leave him: sentenced to life in prison, and fantasizing himself on-screen, in the person of John Travolta.

The book goes on for about another fifty pages, but I'm not sure I'll read them now that the fate of the killer has been decided. I suppose probably there is some kind of twist ahead, but I'm not so fond of twists in mystery novels.

There was a bookstore in the shopping mall. When we dropped in to browse, my friend noticed before I did: Look who's coming to town.

To be precise, it was the next town, at one of the state university's campuses. "How Bad Can It Get." A conference on global crises.

A week from that day, according to the poster.

The wonder of certain coincidences.

Any interest in going? she asked.

I reminded her that I'd already heard that talk. Not to mention having read the article it was based on.

Right, she said. I forgot.

I hope you won't mind my saying I always thought he was a jerk, she added.

One of those aggressive, arrogant, entitled male journal-ists, she called him, reeling off the names of several other conformers to the type.

Nevertheless, he was the one I had turned to. He was the one to whom I'd told everything. He was the one I'd be calling when this whole ordeal was over. But I don't say any of this.

My friend, who is probably the best-read person I know, has been having trouble reading. Ever since my diagnosis, she said. The only time in her life when she wasn't in the middle of several books at once and all eager to move on to new ones.

She had tried turning to books she'd already read, she told me, the ones that had meant the most to her.

But the old magic just isn't there, she said. My favorite writers, my favorite books—they don't affect me like they did before. I don't have the patience. It's really not so dif-ferent from reading *bad* stuff, you know. The way I keep wanting to say, *Why are you telling me all this?*

I tell her about another writer, who wrote on a literary journal's blog about a visit to a former professor whose pas-sion for modern literature had inspired and helped shape the writer when he was a student. Now wheelchair-bound and with much time on his hands, the professor reported that he'd been rereading modern masters—Faulkner, Heming-way, Scott Fitzgerald, and so on. To the writer's question How did they hold up? the old man replied that they did not. Like completely empty performances, he judged them. *Not worth it at all.*

But it's not just reading, my friend said. It's hard for me to know what I should pay attention to anymore. It's been very strange with music, for example. I used to like listening to different kinds of music, she said, but now it's become something of an irritant. Who'd have thought?

Most pop songs sounded drearily the same to her, she said. And the inanity of the lyrics (Why no exceptions to this rule, ever? she asked), which had never really bothered her before, now depressed her.

And lately a lot of classical music also seemed to depress her, she said. It was too much. Too serious, too moving. Too, too unbearably sad, she said.

I was startled to hear this. Recently, classical music had begun unsettling me in much the same way. Music I once loved and considered a blessing and a balm I could no longer listen to, a change I didn't at all understand but that I found heartbreaking.

The owners of the house had a passion for old films. Among their large collection of DVDs was *Make Way for Tomorrow*, a film neither of us had seen before. I was eager to see it when I remembered that it had been an inspiration for Ozu's great film *Tokyo Story*.

The Depression. Having lost their house and all their savings, an elderly couple are forced to turn for help to their children. They don't want to be a burden; in fact the man makes every effort to remain the breadwinner he'd been all his hardworking life, but finding a job at his age turns out to be impossible. To the children, having to deal with parents in needy old age is a burden indeed, and they do little to hide their resentment. Ma and Pa, happily married for more than fifty years, can't bear the thought of separation, but to the children this is the only fair and workable solution. At first supposedly just temporary, the separation is set to become permanent when Pa is forced to move to the home of a daughter living many miles from where Ma has been placed with a son and his wife. The children have arranged a farewell dinner for their parents, but, devastated by their children's betrayal, and relishing the last day they're given to be together before the man must leave for California, the two decide to skip the dinner and make it a night out on their own. They dine together at the very hotel where they spent their honeymoon. Comes the hour when the old man must catch his train. At the station, though they gamely behave as if it's not the last time they'll ever see each other (Pa will find a job out west, he'll send for Ma, they'll be together again soon, never to be parted), it is only too clear (to them, to us) how their story will end.

The saddest picture ever made, Orson Welles called it.

We watched it sitting side by side on the sofa, choking and clutching at each other like two people hopelessly trying to save each other from drowning.

Which is not to say that we regretted having watched it; no matter how sad, a beautifully told story lifts you up.

The owners of the house were into Buster Keaton. We watched Buster Keaton running downhill, dodging an avalanche of rocks, trying to put his passed-out drunk wife to bed, running from an army of cops, getting tangled up in the ropes of a boxing ring, trying to put his passed-out drunk wife to bed, being bullied by various much larger men, loving and being loved by a big brown cow, trying to put his passed-out drunk wife to bed. We watched Buster Keaton fall down, fall down, and fall down again, we watched the bed collapse under his passed-out drunk wife, and we laughed and laughed, choking and clutching at each other like two people hopelessly trying to save each other from drowning.

My friend had been doing yoga for many years—she'd even once had a part-time job as a yoga instructor. There were two yoga studios in town offering two different kinds of yoga classes, but she had no interest in either of them. Like many other people, she'd been doing yoga mainly to help her stay physically fit. Nothing to do with enlightenment. Whatever people might claim, she said, she herself had never witnessed any spiritual growth, any improvement in the moral character of any person she'd known who did yoga—and the number of people she'd known who did yoga was vast—she had never seen anyone who could be said to have become a better person by doing yoga, she said, unless being a better person meant feeling better about yourself; if anything, she said, she had seen people become increasingly self-centered, something she'd seen also in some people who were in psychotherapy. In any case, she didn't have to care about being fit anymore. Since her diagnosis the only exercise she enjoyed was walking. Depending on how well she felt, we took walks around town or through the nature preserve, though there were days when she had to go very slowly and days when she had to stop and sit and rest along the way. Usually we went out together, though sometimes when I got up in the morning she was already out, on her own. She was often up very early, before the light; I had the impression sometimes she'd been up all night, though she insisted that she was in fact sleeping quite well. No fear of losing consciousness, no fear of the dark, so common among people facing death. It was because she wasn't afraid, she thought; it was because she was ready to go. She had discovered that, unlike the pleasure of music, the pleasure of birdsong had not diminished. It was one of the things that drew her out to the nature preserve in the early hours. There'll be birdsong in heaven, she said, if heaven exists.

I wasn't interested in yoga either, but I sought out the nearest gym, a sports club located in the same shopping mall as the bookstore, where I was told I could pay to work out without buying a membership as long as I did so with one of their personal trainers. If I came around the same hour each time, I could work with the same trainer. I would have much preferred to be on my own. I don't like having someone standing by watching and counting so that I can't quietly think my own thoughts while exercising, and the personal trainers I see working at my regular gym often look so bored.

The trainer, though all tattooed tight muscle, had the face of a choirboy and a choirboy's pure treble.

We got off to a bad start when he addressed me as "young lady." Even after he learned my name, he sometimes called me young lady. But there was an earnestness about him that I liked, and he never looked bored. And, after registering the terseness and evasiveness with which I responded to the questions he asked me about myself, he stopped trying to draw me out and we got through our thirty-minute sessions without chatter.

Have you ever done burpees?

I had.

Think you can do ten in thirty seconds?

I could.

Well, that was impressive. You're pretty strong, young lady.

I was also pretty winded. As I was catching my breath I remembered what my friend had said, about her fear that being in such good physical shape would only make her death throes more agonizing. It sank in then, like a spear. No hope, death near, the mind wanting only release, and the body, with a mind of its own, desperately struggling to stay alive, the weakening heart with every beat panting no, no, no.

How terrible. How cruel. How absurd.

Is something wrong? asked the trainer.

I shook my head, but then immediately blurted that a friend of mine was dying.

I'm sorry, he said. Is there anything I can do? Said it reflexively, as people always do, this formula that nobody really wants to hear, that comforts nobody. But it was not his fault that our language has been hollowed out, coarsened, and bled dry, leaving us always stupid and tongue-tied before emotion. A high school teacher once made us read Henry James's famous letter to his grief-stricken friend Grace Norton, held up since its publication as a sublime example of sympathy and understanding. Even he begins by saying, "I hardly know what to say."

Let's sit down, my trainer said. And we did, we sat down together on one of the thick padded exercise mats on the floor.

I wish I could give you a hug, he said. But we're not allowed to touch clients anymore. The manager is afraid of a lawsuit or whatever. It's a problem, because it can be hard to make corrections and explain things like proper alignment with just words. And touch is so important.

My face was in my towel now. My shoulders were jerking.

So you'll just have to imagine it, he said. Imagine my arms around you right now in a big warm hug. His voice cracked. I'm sorry, he said. Ever since I was a kid, I can't not cry when I see someone else crying.

That's because you're still a kid, I said without speaking.

After we had each collected ourselves he said, It's so good that you're working out. Exercise is the best medicine for stress. And please know that I'm always here for you.

But after that day I would not go back. In fact, it would be a very long time before I could bring myself to work out again.

When we were saying goodbye he said, I'm so sorry for what you're going through. Promise me you won't forget about self-care.

I closed my eyes so that he would not see me roll them.

I was in the parking lot when I heard him shrill my name.

I'm sorry, he said as he jogged up to me. I just couldn't let you go like that. Then, after a quick look around to make sure no one was watching, he gave me a big warm hug.

On the way back to the house I imagined myself sharing this story with my friend, before I caught myself and realized that I could not do that.

I don't know who it was, but someone, maybe or maybe

not Henry James, said that there are two kinds of people in the world: those who upon seeing someone else suffering think, That could happen to me, and those who think, That will never happen to me. The first kind of people help us to endure, the second kind make life hell.

III

Off to the gym, I told my friend. Back soon.

In truth, I was meeting my ex. We had arranged to have brunch at one of the town's waterside restaurants the morning after his event at the conference.

When I asked him how it had gone, he shrugged.

"They weren't happy about my not taking questions. Someone said it would be seen as cowardly. There was a time when that would've mattered to me."

"No more?"

"Nevermore."

"You don't care what people think about you anymore."

"Of course I do. But, like most people, I've spent way too much time caring about what other people think of me. My image. My reputation. I'm not sure they ever really mattered, or at least not as much as I thought they did. Not that I can't name far stupider things I've wasted half my life thinking about. I'm obsessed these days with the kinds of things people are paying attention to in spite of the elephant herd in the room. I get a kick out of the *New York Times* home page, scrolling down from the ghastly headlines to their better living feature or whatever it's called: How to have better posture. How to clean your bathroom. How to pack a school lunch."

"*Smarter* living." There have been times in my life when focusing on things like cleaning the bathroom helped keep me sane. There have been times when everything seemed to hinge on whether or not I could get the smallest chore done. Times when nothing meant more than that moment in the day when I took my break from work, found a quiet place, and ate the sandwich and piece of fruit I'd packed that morning. A moment of peace. Anxiety and depression held at bay. I could do it, then. I could live another day.

"I admit that my own interest in things has been shrinking for years," my ex said. "I haven't read a novel in, oh, I can't even say how long. In fact, the only books I read now are for work. I watch a little television when I'm too exhausted to do anything else. But I never go to the movies anymore. No museums, no concerts. No vacations, needless to say. No travel except for work."

For decades it was art and culture he'd gone around the world lecturing about. How could he have lost interest completely?

"If every poet in the world sat down today and wrote a poem about climate change, it wouldn't save one tree. Anyway, art—great art seems to me a thing of the past."

"That's ridiculous. There are more professional artists working now than ever before."

"To be sure. But a certain kind of artistic genius doesn't seem to occur anymore. We're in the age of great tech, where genius abounds, but the last creative artist on a level with, say, Mozart or Shakespeare was George Balanchine, who was born in 1904. In any case, I certainly don't believe in the salvific power of art as I once did. I mean, who could? Considering what we've come to."

"What about sex?"

"What?"

"Going back to what you said about your lack of interest in things that used to matter to you."

"Oh. That, too," he said. "A relief, frankly. A lot of men spend most of their lives going around feeling like dogs. When I look back, if I'm honest I'd say that on the whole my sex life was more degrading than satisfying to me. If there'd been a drug to kill my libido I would've taken it, at least during my wilder years. It would have made me a better person. Anyway, I've become something of a monomaniac, it's true. These days I only write and lecture about one thing. Even if it does make me feel like Cassandra. Even if people do hate me so much that they make death threats. Thank God I'm single now and living alone. But it's not just strangers, you know. A lot of friends have dropped me. My own son is barely speaking to me because I didn't hide how appalled I was that his wife is expecting their third child. Doesn't want me anywhere near her. Says I'm enough to scare her into a miscarriage."

"So you already have two grandchildren. I didn't know that."

"Two boys, five and three."

How do others deal with it. For years you share a life, the same house, the same bed, the same (or so you dare to believe) future plans. You spend so much time together, rarely make a move without consulting the other, reach a point where it's hard to say where one of you ends and the other begins—

"Do you have any photos?"

—and then, incredibly within the same lifetime (and how short, after all, is that) comes a day when you know nothing of even the most important details of the other one's life.

"Of course. But I know you don't really want to see them, you're just being polite."

That time on the subway: wondering why on earth that man was smiling at me, until he leaned forward and said his name. A dozen years earlier, fresh out of school, we'd set up house together. Somehow I had failed to recognize this great love of my life (now married, it turned out, and a new father) sitting across from me on the uptown express.

"But that must be very painful for you, given how pessimistic you are about their future."

Was it that he had changed so much, or that I had buried him so deep, six feet under my heart.

"Unbearable."

Another time, another ex. Catching sight of him through the window of a pizzeria. Too busy with his phone to notice as I stood staring in, swept back to the years of passion and grief. *The lost years*, as I had come bitterly to lament them. Staring in, not caring that I'd attracted the curiosity of several diners, I want to know, why don't I feel more. I want to know how, where once was everything, nothing could be.

In the most romantic movie ever made, a girl yearns for her boyfriend, away at war, even as she finds herself forgetting his face. I would have died for him, she says. How is it that I am not dead?

The saddest musical of all time, one critic called it. *The Umbrellas of Cherbourg.*

"And you really think there's no hope."

And years later, riding the train to visit a friend in Philadelphia, through the gap between the two seats in front of me I recognized his hand, his right hand (all I could see) holding a book. Should I speak to him? No. Nor did I move to another car. Just rode along behind him, wondering, Why don't I feel more. Remembering very well, though, what I *had* felt. The love. The hate. The promise made: Never again. Never again will I allow my life to be spliced with another person's life—

"You've heard what I think," he said. "Read the science

and see what the world is doing about it. Could it be any simpler? Keep releasing carbon into the air and sooner or later—and more and more it's looking like sooner—we're fucked. And make no mistake, if there is in fact even a sliver of hope it depends on the survival of liberal democracy. Nothing is going to hasten the end of a livable planet faster than the rise of the far right. And behold, here they are, the two specters marching side by side."

"But you know," I said, "this idea of yours about people not having children. Wouldn't the next logical step be for people to start killing themselves? I mean because everything we do, really, is contributing to the problem. Every time we turn on a light, or get in a car, or do most anything at this point, we're using up resources, we're polluting the earth, we're destroying other species and dooming our descendants. If enough of us made the sacrifice by taking ourselves out—wouldn't that help?"

"Not going to happen, obviously."

"Any more than people are going to stop having kids."

"Though it will come to that."

"What?"

"People killing themselves to escape the heat and the scarcity of food and clean water. Many will do it before it comes to that."

"Would you ever do that?"

"I don't think I have it in me. I think most people don't, even if they think they do. In any case, barring nuclear war, our generation—the very ones who might have prevented this catastrophe—will be spared the worst."

"I just read a review of a book about some lab worker who purposely unleashes a pandemic flu virus in the hopes of killing enough humans to save the environment."

"Oh yeah? And how did that work out for the environment?"

"The reviewer didn't say. You know, not wanting to be a spoiler."

"Some jerk made a joke about *me* being a spoiler. 'Oh shoot,' he tweeted, 'now we know how life on earth ends.' I think that was supposed to be witty."

"Just sarcastic, I think."

"I'm reporting the *facts*. Why should so much of the response be so hostile to me?"

"It's your attitude," I said. "You come across as cranky and arrogant—bullying, even. And you can't just get up there and tell people there's no hope."

"You mean the truth? Because you can't seriously believe people are going to get their shit together and turn things around in the dozen or so years we've got before we reach the point of no return."

"I don't know. But there's something about the way you present the awful truth, almost as if you took pleasure in it, as if it gave you some kind of grim satisfaction. In other words, your misanthropy shows through."

He laughed. "My defense mechanism, you mean. You

can't seriously believe I take any pleasure in imagining the suffering in store for my grandchildren. But it's true, I do feel pretty hostile myself. All other issues aside, who could ever forgive those Americans—and I'm talking about all the privileged, well-educated ones—who elected a climate change denialist to the world's most powerful office, or the oil CEOs who covered up their own research about the connection between fossil fuels and global warming way back when something might have been done about it. The enormity of that surpasses all the world's episodes of genocide, in my view. I don't know about you, but I've completely lost faith in people to do the right thing."

"But you must have some hope or you wouldn't keep speaking out."

"It's a contradiction, I know. I guess I want at least to be able to look my grandchildren in the eye when they're old enough to ask me where were *you*, what did *you* do. And even if I know there's no longer any hope of waking up idiot humanity in time, why shouldn't they have to hear the truth? Why shouldn't they at least have to think, if only for the time it takes to read an article or listen to a talk, about their own monstrous stupidity and the evil they might have stopped but didn't. The truth is, every time I see a newborn now my heart sinks. I feel terribly angry but also terribly guilty all the time. I'm doing what I'm doing now because I didn't do more before. I wasted my life on things that, no matter how important seeming at the time, turned out to have been trivial."

"And you say that you can't—or won't—forgive others, but you want forgiveness for yourself."

"Yes. From them. I want my grandchildren to forgive me."

At that moment a woman wearing a canvas twin carrier, one infant on her bosom, the other on her back, entered the restaurant—a sight that my ex, sitting with his back to the door, was thankfully spared.

"All that said," he said, "that was one delicious croissant."

One of your favorite things, I said without speaking.

And you always went for the chocolate ones, he nevertheless said back.

Only now did the conversation turn to my friend.

"I know she never liked me," he said. "Whenever we were in the same room, I could feel it. But I respected her. She was a good journalist. Sorry to be using the past tense."

"She wouldn't mind," I said, certain that this was so.

"I've never had any doubt that she's doing the right thing," he said. "It's what I'd hope to be strong enough to do in her place. And you're doing the right thing too—and a really brave thing, in my opinion," he added. "But I can't imagine what you must be going through."

And how could I ever describe it?

I told him the story of how my friend had left the pills behind and we'd had to drive all the way back.

"I shouldn't laugh," he said.

"She wouldn't mind," I told him again.

"There've been quite a few slapstick moments," I said. "Her forgetting to bring the pills, and then this thing that happened a couple of days ago. As I told you, her plan is not to let me know exactly when she'll be taking the pills. One day you'll wake up and it will be done, she said. You'll know because the door to my room will be closed. She always sleeps with the bedroom door ajar, a habit she got into when she had cats, and sleeping in a closed room tends to make her feel claustrophobic, she said. So, that morning I got up earlier than usual—it was still dark—and saw that her door was closed. What did I do? I panicked. I was afraid I was going to faint. I went to the kitchen and threw up in the sink. Then I poured a glass of water, but my mouth was working so violently I couldn't drink it. I sat down at the kitchen table and broke down. I kept trying over and over to get a hold of myself, but I couldn't. I did finally manage to drink the water. I'm not sure how much time passed, it couldn't have been very much, but it had started to get light out. And all of a sudden I hear a noise, and the next thing she's strolling into the kitchen. It turns out she'd had the window open— a rare thing, because she's always cold, especially at night, no matter how steamy it is out there—and sometime during the night the wind blew the fucking door shut."

"I know I shouldn't laugh," he said again, "but it does sound a little like a sitcom. *Lucy and Ethel Do Euthanasia*."

"Oh, believe me, we laughed about it too," I said. "In fact, no one would believe the amount of laughter that's gone on in that house since we got there. But that was only later. At the time, I didn't think it was funny at all. At the time, I was literally shaking with rage. I wanted to break everything in the house, but I settled for throwing the water glass against a wall."

"And how did she respond to that?"

"Totally cool. All she said was 'Do you really think it's fair for you to be mad at me for still being alive?' And then of course you can imagine how I felt. But as I say, we did laugh about it later. It's amazing how she's managed to keep her sense of humor. She even managed to see a silver lining. Think of it as a run-through, she said. Now that you know what it's going to be like, you'll be prepared."

Even though I had thought it many times, *Dying becomes her* was not something I could bring myself to say out loud.

"I've known her all these years and I can tell you no one would ever have called that woman easy," I said. "I was so worried about what being with her would be like. As it turns out, we get along so well, it's like we've always lived together. What?"

"Nothing."

"That look on your face—"

"You just brought me back, that's all. It was a long time ago, but if you don't remember, you once said that to me."

"I don't remember," I said. Though I did.

"Right after we started living together," he said. "That first studio apartment. After a week or so, you said it was like we'd always been together. I'm sorry, I didn't mean to change the subject. Will it be much longer, do you think?"

"No. Soon. Any day."

"How can you be so sure?"

"I can just tell." Again, how to explain it? "I've become attuned to her in the most incredible way. I'll be just about to ask her if she wants something to drink and she'll say, Would you mind getting me some orange juice? I reach for the remote and at the very same instant she says, Can we change the channel?"

It happened all the time. Every day the atmosphere in the house was a little different, a little more charged in some indefinable way, and I had learned to read it. Any day now. I couldn't explain it, but I could tell.

"I know we've already discussed this," he said, "but you do need to remember to take some precautions. She has to leave a note." (In fact, that note, already composed, lay in a drawer of her nightstand, lacking only the date. All part of her meticulous planning.) "And there shouldn't be any evidence that could be construed as your having been part of the plan, or of having assisted in any way. No one knows, right, besides the three of us? Make sure it stays that way. She's right, maybe it's good that you had this little 'run-through.' You've got to keep it together. Don't go spilling your guts when the police arrive. They'll check out the house very carefully. They'll ask you questions. You stick to the script. And you should call the police first, before you call me."

"I have to call her daughter too," I said. "I should call her before I call you."

"All right. But be careful what you say."

"This is insane." My eyes and throat were stinging. "I don't understand why we have to go through all this, as if we were criminals, for God's sake. Why shouldn't dying people have the right to end their own lives?"

"They will—once there are so many old and terminally ill people that they threaten to knock our teetering health care system out completely. Your doctor will write you a prescription, it will be cheap and easy to fill, and it will all be perfectly legal. No more having to go to the dark web."

"You really think that's going to happen?"

"It's the only practical solution—and the only compassionate one, in my view."

Except that most people won't choose it. Was our joint unspoken thought.

We know that the belief that it is ethically wrong for human beings to procreate isn't new. In fact, it is ancient. Life is suffering, birth feeds death, to bring a person who has no say in the matter into this world is morally unjustifiable, goes the anti-natalist philosophy. That life might also bring an individual a great amount of pleasure changes nothing, the anti-natalists say. Unborn, the person would not have missed life's pleasures. Born, he or she has no choice but to endure its multitude of physical and emotional pains, such as the pain that comes from aging or disease or dying. The possibility of a happier future, in which suffering would be vastly diminished, cannot be a justification for the suffering that exists today. And in any case, according to a leading contemporary anti-natalist, a happier future is an illusion. The main problem was, is, and ever will be human nature, the anti-natalist says. Everything could have been different, true. But that would have required us to be a different species. Humans don't learn. They make the same terrible mistakes over and over, he says. "We're asked to accept the unacceptable. It's unacceptable that people, and other beings, have to go through what they go through, and there's almost nothing that they can do about it."

When he's asked whether or not he has any children, the anti-natalist won't say.

IV

Later, I found myself confessing the truth, that I'd gone not to the gym that morning but to meet my ex, and that in spite of the promise of silence I'd made her I had told him everything.

A week ago, maybe, that would've bothered her, she said. She didn't ask me why I'd changed my mind.

Time. We were both keenly aware that it had become a different element from what it had been before we crossed the threshold of that house.

So strange, she'd said earlier, on one of our walks. Sometimes it feels as if we'd been here for years.

I knew what she meant. Within a week our relationship had grown to such a degree that it eclipsed the friendship of our youth. And it was this new intimacy that made secrets and lies intolerable.

I never liked him, she said. But if he's really as tormented as he sounds, I am sorry for him. How sad to be wishing your own grandchildren had never been born. Though to be honest, I'm glad I don't have any grandchildren of my own to worry about.

Perhaps another thing the dystopian future might bring: People suing their parents for having given them birth. Pointing as evidence to the abundance of scientific studies and warnings their parents had been given. *What did you assholes* think *two minutes to midnight meant?*

Sometimes, without my asking, without my saying a word, my friend answered the very question that was on my mind. She would turn her gaze back from the window, through which she'd been watching birds at the feeding pole that we filled twice a day, or she'd look up from the book she'd been trying—usually unsuccessfully—to read, and she would speak.

I miss childhood, she said. I was a happy kid, and I'm grateful for that, because so many people I've known had a hard time growing up. But I see myself walking home from the bus stop, swinging my little brown leather book bag, one of my favorite possessions ever, how I wish I had kept it—how I wish I could touch it now—and singing one of the songs we'd learned that week. I loved music hour! The teacher would put on a record and we'd listen and then she'd teach us the song and we'd sing it at the top of our lungs, the gifted and the tone-deaf all cheerfully together. It makes a particular kind of sound, if you've ever noticed, that mix of unequal voices, no doubt unpleasant to many ears, but all my life it's given me goose bumps to hear the sound of children singing, especially when they do it badly. When they do it well, when it's a serious performance, something they've rehearsed, they sound like angels, she said, but they don't sound as free or as happy to me, they're not having as much fun.

That beloved schoolbag, she went on, and its precious contents: the black-and-white Mead composition book, the loose-leaf binder with the subject dividers with the candy-colored tabs, the pens and pencils, the pencil sharpener, the eraser, the ruler and the protractor and the pencil compass— all of which made me feel so important. School, in general, made me feel loved. I can remember the feeling very clearly, she said, even if I couldn't have put it into words. That some-body wanted to teach me things, that they cared about my penmanship, my stick-figure drawings, the rhymes in my poems. That was love. That was most surely love, she said. Teaching is love. And in some ways that love meant more to me than the love of my parents, because my parents exagger-ated every tiny good thing, neither my mother nor my father was ever critical, they praised everything equally, she said, every effort I made, and if I did poorly they blamed the test or assignment for being too hard. Unlike my teachers they made no distinction between effort and achievement, she said, but I wasn't fooled, I knew I couldn't trust what they said, so it was the teachers' opinions that really mattered. In any case, mine weren't the kind of parents who want to be all involved in their kid's education. That was the school's job, as they saw it. I know many kids learn how to read early, at home. But for me that momentous event—that most important rung of my life—didn't happen till school.

I can name every teacher I had in grade school, she said, starting with kindergarten: Miss Gillings, Mrs. Matthews, Miss Lopez, Miss Banks, Mr. Goldenthal, Mrs. Hershey, Mr. Cork. I loved them all. I loved all my teachers when I was a kid. Even the ones I'd come to understand later were not really so good as they'd seemed to me—were in fact pretty bad at their jobs. I still remember them fondly, she said.

(Here I am reminded of a conversation I once had with a man who'd graduated just a few years before from a college where I myself once taught. When asked with whom he'd studied there, he could not recall a single name.)

My memory is that I was not unusual, my friend said. My memory is that most of my classmates liked school too. But I remember also bad moments, children getting upset, children in pain. I remember being baffled by one girl in particular. Winnie. "Winnie the Poop." Everyone disliked her, even the teacher didn't hide his dislike for this girl, but it wasn't clear to me what was so bad about her. Her mother really did dress her funny, though, like an orphan in an illustration in a Victorian novel, dark, solid-colored shapeless dresses way down past her knees—now I think they must have been homemade and all cut from the same pattern—and these clunky, orthopedic-looking oxfords. But she never bothered anyone, she kept to herself, she sat slumped down low in her seat, clearly trying to be invisible. But every now and then, for no reason that we could tell, in the middle of class, while the teacher was talking or writing something on the board, this hideous sound, this animal yowl, would go up and we'd all turn to see her sitting there, her head thrown back and her mouth wide open, clenching and unclenching her fists, sobbing. A terrible sight, but at the same time so weird, so comical, it must be said, that some kids would laugh.

I was shocked but also mesmerized, my friend said. I was such a protected child—what did I know about suffering? And I remember how bad I felt for her. In fact, I've always thought of this as my first real experience of pity. I remember how strange it was, the way it seemed to be both a bad feeling and a good feeling at the same time—how was that? And it was more than just feeling sorry for someone—that was something I'd felt often enough before. This was something bigger, and it demanded some kind of action.

A chance to act nobly! I could not have been more delighted. I would befriend this pathetic, unhappy little outcast. And so high was my opinion of myself that I believed the honor and blessing of my attention was all that was needed to change her life. Oh, I remember how thrilled I was to feel these chivalrous impulses tickling my spine.

But instead of accepting, let alone reciprocating, my gestures of friendship, Winnie was hostile to me. One day when I'd taken the pass to use the girls' room, she went into my book bag. Though I knew what she'd done—she couldn't resist smirking at me when I returned to class—when the teacher asked us to take out our notebooks, rather than accuse Winnie of stealing I let myself be punished for having "lost" mine. Curiously enough, it was right after this that Winnie decided she wanted us to be friends after all. Talk about punishment! The class was too kind: she really was a drag, the first chronic depressive I ever met, she must have been, not a lively bone in her body, not a song in her heart or a dream in her head. Winnie the Poop! Being with her was like being trapped in a dark moldy cellar. For the rest of that school year, she clung to me and so, unfortunately, like slime, did the thing that made other kids want nothing to do with her. It was either her or my other friends, but it wasn't as simple as choosing my other friends. I just wasn't capable of doing what needed to be done to get rid of her—not when I'd been the one to initiate the friendship. I was too ashamed, and I was so relieved when, at the start of the next school year, she and I ended up in different classes.

You go back, my friend said. Your mind takes you back. There's a key, or you think there's a key. A hand in your mind reaches out— Oh but you must be so tired of hearing me go on like this.

No, go on. I'm listening. I want to know. Go on.

I miss childhood, she said. When I was in third grade, a boy fell in love with me. He even proposed. I mean it! During recess one day he went down on one knee and said, Will you marry me? And I said, Where's the ring? There's supposed to be a ring. And some other kids had gathered around and they all started laughing at him. For a week or so he went around looking pissed, not talking to me or anyone else. And then one day he did it again, went down on one knee—and pulled out a ring. Such a ring! The most beautiful sparkly thing, but it was too big for me. I was going to wear it on a chain around my neck, but it turned out he'd stolen it—it was his big sister's engagement ring! Thank God I didn't lose it.

There's a certain kind of happiness, my friend said, that is open only to young children. I mean, as a child, it's possible to be totally focused on just one thing. It's your birthday. You asked for a bike, or a puppy, or a new pair of skates. As the day draws near it's all you can think about. And then it happens, your wish fulfilled, your dream come true, and nothing to spoil it. In getting that one thing it's as if you'd been given everything. But after a certain age, that feeling— that pure bliss—doesn't happen, it can't happen, because you never want just one thing anymore, once you reach puberty it's no longer possible.

(Now I am reminded of a friend's little girl whose heart's desire was to have a Barbie doll. For a while her mother, who disapproved of the sexualized doll, resisted. Then, one Christmas, she gave in. When she had lifted her out of the box, the enraptured six-year-old in a passionate voice declared: Barbie! I love you! I have always loved you!)

For me, said my friend, the first day of school was the happiest day of the year. I remember being so excited that I couldn't sleep the night before. We went to church every Sunday, but for me school was the true holy place, the place of hope and thankfulness and joy. The worship of God once a week was completely abstract, but the love of learning—that was real.

But I want to know, she said, why couldn't it have been the same for my daughter? Why wasn't I capable of giving her a childhood more like my own? And my parents, who played such a big part in her upbringing, my mother especially—why did the two of us grow up so unlike? I remember that as a kid I was tolerant, I was fair-minded. I liked everyone, I was never mean, I played well with others, I knew how to share, I knew how to listen. So why did I grow up to be so impatient? How often has it been said of me that I don't suffer fools. And it's true, I don't, and it always made me proud to hear that. But when I think how uncritical and forgiving and coddling my parents always were—why was I, as an adult, as a parent, not like that too? And for all my love of school and fond memories of teachers, I myself hated teaching, I avoided teaching as much as I could, and whenever I did teach I was nothing like my old teachers, I was not a good teacher myself, I had no patience with students—just as I had no patience with my classmates in college and grad school, and as I've never had any patience with most of my colleagues. *Cold. Intimidating. Condescending. Bullying. Professor from Hell. Bitch.* Those were the kinds of things my students wrote about me in their course evaluations. And rather than care, I just stopped reading them. But now I can't stop wondering, when I look back, when I remember my teachers, when I remember all that happiness and love, why did I myself scorn teaching my whole adult life?

I'm losing my voice, she said. (She had been talking nonstop for hours.) And you must be sick of hearing it.

I shook my head. In fact, I was riveted. Indeed, so riveted was my attention on her every word that it felt almost as if there were something indecent about it.

I don't think I ever told you this story, she began one time. No, she hadn't, but I knew it anyway, or at least the version of it that rumor had circulated. When she was still a teenager, her daughter had come between her and a man.

Can you imagine anything more sordid, my friend said. Your daughter making a play for your boyfriend. And right under your nose too. And he was so flattered, the fool. I had to ban him from our lives before the unspeakable happened. I even threatened him with the police. And once he was gone she forgot all about him. It wasn't as if she'd really cared, of course. She wasn't some helpless innocent. All she'd wanted was to hurt me. And she wanted as many people as possible to know about it too, so I'd have to suffer the greatest possible humiliation.

That's when she understood how much her own child hated her, my friend said.

She had never got over it. A stain on her life that could never be washed out, she described it. A sorrow that could arise unexpectedly at any moment, and that did seem to arise at particularly happy or peaceful moments, she said—to ruin them.

I'd be having a perfectly good day, going about my business, when suddenly for no clear reason the memory of it all would come back, and I'd be forced to relive it. I learned that I could get past it by burying myself in my work, but there were times when it was enough to sink me into a depression for days.

But didn't they ever try to talk about it? I asked. I meant when her daughter had grown older.

They did, she said. And got absolutely nowhere.

Her daughter's memory of the incident was quite different. In her view, she was hardly the guilty one. She was just a kid, after all. It was the man's fault, she said. He was a creep, but her mother had been too infatuated to see it. She had only herself to blame for bringing a guy like that into their lives in the first place.

Much later, she would say that her mother had overreacted. If it had been as big a deal as her mother seemed to think, surely it would have stayed with her, the daughter said. But in fact she couldn't recall which of her mother's boyfriends they were even talking about. And later still, she insisted that her mother had misremembered everything. Between her and this guy, whoever he was, nothing had happened.

You want to forgive all, my friend said, and you should forgive all. But you discover that some things you can't forgive, not even when you know you're dying. And then that becomes its own open wound, she said: the inability to forgive.

V

Have you noticed, she said. Her face has changed.

She was talking about the portrait in the living room. We had grown more than used to it. No longer an eyesore, it had become a mysteriously comforting presence. She seemed to be watching over us, we agreed.

Like a spirit, my friend said.

Like the household saint.

The expression on her face has changed, my friend insisted. She looks sadder.

No, not exactly sadder, I said. But maybe softer. The first time I saw her I thought she looked a bit stern.

She disapproved of us before. Now she's accepted us.

She's gotten to know us better. Now she likes us.

It is soothing, my friend said, to look at her. If you keep staring at her eyes, it calms you.

Put a halo on her, I said, and she'd look like an icon.

Beneath the portrait stood a narrow marble-topped table. One day my friend placed a candle there and a small pewter vase of wildflowers she had picked.

You've made a shrine, I said. It makes me want to pray to her.

Let us pray.

I dreamed that I was asleep, my friend said, and in my dream I opened my eyes and saw her standing by the bed, bending over me.

It wasn't a dream. I saw her too.

Maybe you could read to me for a while, she said. I've never liked audiobooks, but now, when I can't read myself, it's nice to be read to.

I asked her what she wanted me to read, and she pointed to the paperback splayed on the coffee table, where I'd left it days ago.

I love mysteries, she said. I used to read one or two a week. You don't have to start from the beginning, just summarize what's happened so far.

In the last part of the book, the narrative switches from third to first person. Speaking now is the budding actress, and we learn that everything we've read so far has been her

fictionalization of events taken from life. The book, written under a masculine pseudonym, is about to be published.
Now we learn about her life in the three decades since her
relationship with the serial killer: how that experience had
traumatized her to the point that she was barely able to func-
tion let alone continue pursuing her once-so-promising acting career. And it turns out there was more, much horrible
more to the story.

After being dumped by the killer, the actress's best friend
discovers she is pregnant. By the time she learns that the father of the child she is carrying is a psychopathic murderer,
it's too late to consider an abortion. She hatches a plan to
conceal her condition for the remainder of her term and give
birth at home, in secret. She enlists the help of a close male
friend, together with whom she withdraws to a rural hideout. The plan is to abandon the newborn in a safe place, its
parents' identity remaining forever unknown and untrace-
able. But things go awry, and the baby dies two days after he
is born. By this time the young man, besieged by fears and
regrets about his collusion, has begged the narrator to come
to the hideout and try to persuade their friend, now seriously
depressed and behaving irrationally, to see a doctor. Thus
the narrator is a witness to the baby's death. To this day, she
tells us, she has never been sure whether he died of crib death
or some other natural cause or was in fact smothered by his
emotionally troubled mother. But when, in order to protect
her friend and the young man (and, by extension, herself)

from what would likely be a criminal investigation—one that could quite possibly lead to a murder charge—she agrees to maintain silence about the infant, whose body the man goes off alone to bury in the woods.

In the final pages we learn that, while the baby's mother went on to have something of a normal life, the young man, unable to live with the burden of guilt and secrecy, killed himself. The narrator is on the verge of getting married to someone she describes as the love of her life. She has told this person the full story of the serial killer but nothing of the rest. The day of the big wedding is near. The book ends with her pondering whether she can allow her beloved to marry her without knowing the whole truth. She decides to make a full confession, knowing that it may well cause her to lose her one last chance at happiness.

Hah, said my friend. A twist. Ends supposedly happily with a wedding but then sets up a cliff.

According to my high school English teacher, there are two kinds of novels. Half of them could be called *Crime and Punishment* and the other half could be called *A Love Story*. But when you think about it, a lot of novels could be both.

Crime and Punishment: A Love Story. Now that's a good title. Anyway, don't they say that every good story is a suspense story?

And every story is a love story.

And every love story is a ghost story.

And everybody loves somebody sometime.

Stop! she squealed. It hurts when I laugh that hard. (She was referring to her several surgery scars.)

I had some recently published novels on my Kindle, but my friend wasn't interested in listening to any of them. She didn't like what she called the vandalizing streak in contemporary fiction writers. She quoted John Cheever on the difference between a fascinated horror of life and a vision of life.

Nowadays it seems to be mostly fascinated horror, she said. Either that or totally unconvincing platitudinous sentiment.

All these books about the horribleness of modern life, she said, a lot of them brilliant, I know, I know, you don't have to tell me. But I don't want to read any more about narcissism and alienation and the futility of relationships between the sexes. I don't want to read any more about human, in particular male, hideousness. Whatever happened to Faulkner's idea that a writer's job was to lift people up?

How Faulkner chastised the young writer of his day: He writes *as though he stood among and watched the end of man.*

He writes not of the heart but of the glands. It was out of fear that the writer wrote this way, Faulkner said. The fear he shared with every other person on earth: the fear of being blown up. But it was the writer's duty to rise above such fear, Faulkner said. Valor was what Faulkner was calling for, that day in Stockholm, in 1950. And then: a return to *the old universal truths—love and honor and pity and pride and compassion and sacrifice.* Absent which, Faulkner warned, your story will last but a day.

Fine words. Really fine words. But of all the ways of looking at a writer today, as a knight in shining armor strikes me as probably the most far-fetched.

Another time, my friend said to me: You'd think it would be easier to leave life if you could convince yourself that everything was horrible and the future was totally bleak. But I can't bear to think that I'll be gone and the world won't go on, infinitely rich, infinitely beautiful. Take that away and there's no consolation.

I myself, as I told my friend now, have always been haunted by a scene from an old movie I once saw, based on the lives of the Brontë family. One of the sisters, who knows she's dying, says that because she's always been afraid of life, she doesn't so much mind leaving it. But then, on a day like this, she says, when the world is so beautiful (she is sitting somewhere outdoors, I recall, no doubt somewhere in the moors), she confesses that she wouldn't mind living just a little longer.

I'd been channel surfing, and that was the only scene I watched. It was long ago—I could be remembering it wrong. But this was how it always came back to me. And it came back to me a lot.

Meanwhile I was scanning a large bookcase in the living room. How about this, I said, pulling a heavy book from the bottom shelf: *The World's Best Folk and Fairy Tales.*

Gods and heroes, princes and peasants, giants and little people, witches, tricksters, and animals, animals, animals.

This would be our reading from now on. She could not get enough of it. Now I was the one who almost lost her voice.

Much has been said about mystery stories being like fairy tales—and popular for some of the same reasons. Instead of ogres, serial killers. And though they might not be pure of heart—no princes, or Galahads, or saints—the detectives are still heroes, righteous if not always noble avengers. All is simplified. Characters: types. Moral code: clear. Where guilt or innocence lie: plain. Plenty of cruelty, violence, and gore, but in the end the evil are vanquished, and even if the good don't live happily ever after there is closure, the kind of closure that mostly eludes people in real life.

Except that fairy tales are beautiful, my friend said. Fairy tales are sublime, and mysteries are not.

Another difference: unlike mysteries, fairy tales are not escapist. Even if they too simplify and conform to familiar formulas, the truths in fairy tales always run deep. That is why children love them. (Who knows better than a child what it's like to be at the mercy of hidden and arbitrary forces, and that anything can happen, no matter how strange, either for good or for ill.) Fairy tales are real. They are more mysterious than any mystery novel. That is why, unlike mystery novels—meant to entertain, then be forgotten—fairy tales are classics. They are of the heart, not of the glands.

I like that we owe fairy tales to old women. When the idea came to people to collect those of a given region, they began by taking down the tales told by its crones.

What's your favorite fairy tale? my friend wanted to know.

Any one that has swans in it, I said. I remember, when I first read "The Six Swans," how I wanted to be the brother whose magic shirt his sister doesn't have time to finish, so when he's turned back into a human being he still has one wing.

You wanted to be the freak.

Well, I didn't think of it that way. Maybe just the different one, I said. The one who gets to keep part of his swan being. That appealed to me.

Here's something I wonder about, my friend said. They say people love thrillers and horror stories because it's such fun to escape ordinary life and lose yourself in a world of gruesome violence and crime. Yes?

Yes.

So why aren't romance novels full of bad sex with smelly people?

That is not a logical analogy.

Okay, never mind. Chemo brain! Just keep reading.

We had taken to sitting side by side on the sofa when we were together in the living room, semi-recumbent with our legs stretched out and our feet up on the coffee table. She would nestle against me, sometimes letting her head drop to my shoulder. More than once while I was reading she fell asleep. I would stop reading and keep very still, alternately soothed and tormented by the sound of her breathing. I would remember the vigil at my father's hospital bedside, when his breathing had become so labored that it was as if there were some malfunctioning machine in the room, and the shock of it ceasing, like *that*, as if the machine had been switched off, and the silence that followed, louder than his breathing had been, louder than any machine, louder than anything I'd ever heard before in my life.

Or we'd sit together in the same position on the two-seater on the back porch, from where we liked to watch the sunset. Sometimes we linked arms or clasped hands. (*Touch is so important.*) At such moments I felt that she was as much a comfort to me as I was meant to be to her. Every now and then she would squeeze my hand without saying anything—without needing to say anything—but it was as if she had squeezed my heart.

Golden hour, magic hour, *l'heure bleue*. Evenings when the beauty of the changing sky made us both go still and dreamy. Sunlight falling at an angle across the lawn so that it touched our elevated feet, then moved up our bodies like a long slow blessing, and I found myself a breath away from believing that everything was as it should be. See the moon. Count the stars. *There all the time without you: and ever shall be, world without end* (Joyce). Infinitely rich, infinitely beautiful. Everything was going to be all right.

Once as I was turning a page she picked her head up off my shoulder and kissed me. I laughed, startled, then kissed her back. And because she could never pass up an opening for a joke, she whined a pitch-perfect imitation of Bette Davis as Baby Jane: You mean all this time we could've been lovers?

I've been so selfish, she said. I never thought about you. I guess I couldn't allow myself to. But now that we're here, now that all this is happening (*all this*: the inexorable, the inexpressible), I feel guilty.

But I want to be here, I said. And as I said it I realized it was absolutely true. Nothing could have torn me away.

That wasn't what she meant, she said. It's that I feel guilty about leaving you behind.

It happens. It happens when people find themselves caught in some extreme situation, a crisis, an emergency, especially one involving death, or the threat of death, when even total strangers can become intensely close, in some cases developing a lasting bond. Survivors of disasters, or near disasters, thrown together even for just a short time, arrange for annual reunions that go on for years after the experience they shared had occurred. There is the story of two people who met for the first time when the elevator they were in got stuck between floors. By the time they were freed many hours later they had agreed to marry. *And they lived happily ever after.* Well, no. They broke their engagement about a year later, but I believe they remained friends.

I didn't think about you at all, my friend said. I didn't count on having feelings for you, worrying about you.

And the feelings I was having for her—I hadn't counted on those, either.

One of the many oddities of our situation had to do with grocery shopping. My friend's interest in food was so diminished that she didn't like to go shopping at all. The smells inside the supermarket could even sometimes nauseate her. Nor could she stand how freezing cold the store was kept, and the vast size of it—like a fucking airport, she said— exhausted her the minute she entered. (As for me, I am never in one of those megastores without wishing I were on blades.) So I usually went alone. But it was impossible to calculate how much food we'd need without touching on the awful question *For how long.* And so up and down the aisles I went, dazed and shuffling like a hundred-year-old woman.

Also, there was shame. Almost nothing can curb my appetite, and, during this time, for whatever reason (or perhaps for a very obvious reason), I was always hungry. Every meal with my friend ended the same: her plate barely touched, mine clean. I snacked between meals as well. Without getting on a scale I knew that I was gaining weight, and I was ashamed of this. Though I resisted gorging on things like doughnuts and ice cream, I was ashamed of how much I craved them. My greedy appetite seemed to me like an insult to my dying friend. Small wonder that, though the meals I ate were nutritious, they were usually followed by indigestion.

It was while I was at the supermarket one afternoon that my friend, who even on scorching days often suffered from chills, decided to take a hot bath. This particular day she was also suffering more than usual from fatigue. She lay down to wait until the bathtub was filled.

I sloshed across the room to the bed where she sat hugging her knees to her chest, dazed and shivering, like a person adrift on a raft after a shipwreck.

I just wanted to close my eyes for a minute, she said. Teeth chattering.

I climbed onto the bed, tucking my wet feet under me. *Two* persons adrift.

It wasn't supposed to be this way, she said. All I wanted was peace. I wanted to die in peace, and now it's turned into this nightmare. This farce. This hideous, humiliating farce.

Then she was crying so convulsively that she could no longer get the words out. I heard them anyway: She had wanted to be strong. She had wanted control. She had wanted to die on her own terms and with as little trouble to the world as possible. She had wanted peace. She had wanted order.

Peace and order around her was all she had asked for.

A calm, clean, graceful, even—why not?—beautiful death. Was what she'd had in mind.

A beautiful death in a nice house in a scenic town on a fine summer night.

Was the end my friend had written for herself.

It's not your fault, I said. And of course it wasn't my fault, either. So why could I not shake the feeling that, on the contrary, I, and nobody else, was very much to blame?

As I sat trying to comfort her, I was also trying to think about what must be done. How would we ever explain this to our hosts? But hateful as that duty was, it could not be put off. They would need to contact their home insurer immediately.

A couple sits in their living room watching TV when suddenly the ceiling cracks open, releasing a cascade of water from an overflowing bathtub upstairs. As they jump to their feet, clutching their heads in dismay, the house door opens and in marches a crew of smiling, uniformed, attractive young people. Now the homeowners are bewitched into statue-stillness and the team sets to work, cleaning up the mess and fixing everything, good as new. As the door closes behind them, the couple are released from their spell, unaware that anything was ever amiss. *Like it never even happened* is the company's promise. I'd seen their TV commercial many times, and I'd seen their trucks with FIRE AND WATER CLEANUP AND RESTORATION painted on the side, and now, a little dementedly, I kept seeing the commercial in my head, drawing hope from its magic, its fairy-tale ending.

Meanwhile, my friend was rambling. It had been a mistake

to come here, it was a stupid idea. It was a fantasy. She should have known it would go all wrong. It was unfair, it was so fucking unfair.

After a pause she shook me out of my thoughts by shouting, I've never been so unhappy in my life! I hate myself!

To die in despair. The phrase came to me, and all the water in the room turned to ice.

It must not happen. It must not be allowed to happen.

My friend was shrieking now. Oh, what *is* this, what the fuck *is* this.

It was life, that's what. Life going on, in spite of everything. Messy life. Unfair life. Life that must be dealt with. That I must deal with. For if I didn't do it, who would?

PART THREE

Everything that a writer writes could just as easily have been different–but not until it's been written. As a life could have been different, but not until it's been lived.

–Inger Christensen

The journal I had planned to keep, a record of my friend's last days—that never happened. I started it, but almost immediately I stopped. I did not even save the few pages I had written. I discovered that I didn't want to make a written record after all. The reason seemed to be that I had no faith in it. From the beginning it felt like a betrayal—I don't mean of my friend's privacy but of the experience itself. No matter how hard I tried, the language could never be good enough, the reality of what was happening could never be precisely expressed. Even before I began I knew that whatever I might manage to describe would turn out to be, at best, somewhere to the side of the thing, while the thing itself slipped past me, like the cat you never even see escape when you open the house door. We talk glibly about finding the right words, but about the most important things, those words we never find. We put the words down as they must be put down, one after the other, but that is not life, that is not death, one word after the other, no, that is not right at all. No matter how hard we try to put the most important things into words, it is always like toe-dancing in clogs.

Understood: language would end up falsifying everything, as language always does. Writers know this only too well, they know it better than anyone else, and that is why the good ones sweat and bleed over their sentences, the best ones break themselves into pieces over their sentences, because if there is any truth to be found they believe it will be found there. Those writers who believe that the way they write is more important than whatever they may write about—these are the only writers I want to read anymore, the only ones who can lift me up. I can no longer read books that—

But why am I telling you all this?

Language would falsify everything. Why, then, create an inauthentic document, to be taken (*mis*taken) by anyone who later read it—including even myself—for the truth?

Something else: Writing in the journal did not have the steadying or consoling power I'd hoped for. It did not soothe me. It frustrated me instead. It made me feel dumb. Dumb and hopeless. It filled me with anxiety: what a terrible writer I had become.

What if all this time we have misunderstood the story of

the Tower of Babel? My ex once put the question in an essay. Behold the people is one, and they all have one language. Said God, This will not do. As one, the people might actually succeed in building the city and the heavenward tower with which they hoped to make their name. Indeed, the All-Knowing knew that, with a common tongue, *nothing would be impossible for them.* The way to stop this abomination was to replace the one language with many. And so it was done.

But what if God had in fact gone even further. What if it was not just to different tribes but to each individual human being that a separate language was given, unique as fingerprints. And, step two, to make life among humans even more strifeful and confounding, he beclouded their perception of this. So that while we might understand that there are many peoples speaking many different languages, we are fooled into thinking that everyone in our own tribe speaks the same language we do.

This would explain much of human suffering, according to my ex, who was being less playful than you might think. He really did believe that's how it was: each of us languaging on, our meaning clear to ourselves but to nobody else.

Even people in love? I asked, smilingly, teasingly, hopefully. This was at the very beginning of our relationship. He only smiled back. But years later, at the bitter end, came the bitter answer: *People in love most of all.*

———

I once heard a journalist say that whenever he's working on a piece, he knows his language probably isn't clear when he finds himself repeatedly cleaning the computer screen.

Bringing to mind Orwell's ideal of prose as clean and clear as a windowpane.

Look out the window, goes the schoolteacher's writing prompt. What do you see?

When I looked out the window, the monster was still there.

I have not, so far, regretted not having kept the journal, though I suppose one day I might. On the other hand, I find myself thinking about a film called *No Home Movie*, in which the Belgian filmmaker Chantal Akerman documented conversations with her mother during the last months of her mother's life. We should all be great filmmakers.

I understand it's a thing now, people making videos and arranging to have them delivered posthumously to one or more persons whom they knew in life. In some cases the video is intended to be shown at the deceased's memorial service. I'm not sure why, but I find it hard to imagine this being done in any way that doesn't feel cheesy.

The podcast my friend had told me about, the one she'd made at the request of a hospital social worker to answer questions about what it was like to be terminally ill, and which she afterward regretted—as I'd suspected, it's not as bad as she made it sound. I, at least, would not describe it, as she did, as her going "off the rails," even though she made me wince a few times. *What will I miss most? I won't miss anything, I'll be dead. I won't have any feelings.* Brittle little laugh.

She sounds irked. She *is* irked. (*How often has it been said of me that I don't suffer fools.*)

A surprise: asked whether she'd thought of taking her own life, without hesitation she answers no, when in fact we know this thought had been with her from the day of her diagnosis.

Regrets?

Not that she hadn't spent more time with her daughter, not that she hadn't succeeded in making amends with her, but rather that she hadn't had another child (a statement that obviously can be read in two ways).

How she loathes the term *bucket list*. How she prefers *fatal* to *terminal*. Not only does she not believe in an afterlife, she is gobsmacked that so many people do believe in one.

Probably it was her tone that she regretted. She didn't want to appear angry or bitter. To be emotional over your own death was *unbecoming* (her use of that word on the podcast was one winceable moment). To the end, she clung to an image of stoical poise.

Being already there, I get sucked in and listen to the other episodes in the series. No surprise that most of the participants are women (as is the social worker). Aren't women always more willing than men to talk about their feelings? Why wouldn't they be more willing to talk about being ill and what they're going through as they face death. Besides, most of those interviewed are old, and everyone knows how laconic old men tend to be—especially if at some time in their lives they've been to war. Also, it seems to me that, when asked to do something for someone else, women, even if not greatly enthused, are more likely than men to oblige. (There appears to be some controversy about studies, of which there are no few, that involve asking the dying for interviews or to fill out surveys or questionnaires and so on. Is it ethical to take up the time of those to whom so little time remains, ask some.)

What I hear, listening to the podcast, is an extraordinary amount of accord. Whether or not there is acceptance, there is also fear. Fear of pain. Fear of the dark. Even those who do "go gentle" don't seem entirely sure about the "good" part. (It seems the one person with whom the poet could not share his poem was the very one who had inspired it, and who is addressed in it, the reason being that Dylan Thomas's father hadn't been told that he was dying.) Far more anxiety than zen, I hear. Every single one of those interviewed has watched someone die before them. Bucket lists and last wishes are modest. One more Christmas. One more spring. ("I'm hoping for a last vacation with the grandkids" . . . "to make my son's law school graduation" . . . "to finish the renovations on the house.") Several find themselves quite naturally dwelling on the past. ("Mother's face keeps coming back." "The anger I felt all these years about my divorce I don't feel anymore.") Sadness and worry for those left behind, for whom one's death is predicted to be harder than for oneself. ("If only my kids weren't so young." "I'm not sure my husband even knows where the kitchen is, he's gonna starve to death." And what about the cats?)

An absence of self-pity, with the exception of the mother of the young kids. She did everything "right," this woman assures us. She never hurt anyone, she played by all the rules. *She was a good person.* Why her why her why her.

An absence of humor, with the exception of one very raspy-voiced fifty-year-old man who obsesses about his epitaph. He's heard a lot of good ones, he says, his favorite being "See you soon." Can I use one that's already been used before? he asks. Or would that be plagiarism?

As if he might get sued for that.

The Man Who Plagiarized His Epitaph. And Other Poems. My friend would have loved it.

Bucket list comes from *kick the bucket*, of course. But where *kick the bucket* comes from no one seems to know.

What does a bucket have to do with anything? And why *kick* it? And is there supposed to be something *in* the bucket? (My friend.)

I always thought it was about a dying horse. It kicked its bucket when it collapsed. But I can find no source for this.

Any connection to the Russian superstition that seeing someone carrying an empty bucket is a bad omen?

Except for my friend and one other woman, who says simply that she doesn't know, everyone says they believe they will see their loved ones again. Not for the first time, I note that no one ever seems to be afraid of going to Hell. Hell is other people, if you agree with Sartre. Evidently, to most, it's *for* other people, never for yourself. And never for the ones you're looking forward to seeing again. Like the extinction of life on earth as a result of nuclear war or climate change, an afterlife that includes the possibility of never-ending fear and pain appears to be a horror too vast to be assimilable.

Paradise, California, lost. After the Camp Fire had laid waste to the town, one editorialist wrote, "That human imagination envisaged the place of eternal damnation as an inferno and that human folly has created a future of ever-worsening heat waves and wildfires might strike at least some as two hells of a coincidence."

I catch myself wishing—not without guilt—that the podcast was more interesting. Bored by the way they talk about themselves, and feeling shitty about it (though any honest talk therapist will tell you how often they have to fight to stay awake as patients unburden themselves), I can't help suspecting that, rather than say what they really think or feel, these people are saying what they think other people want to hear. Meaning, what is acceptable, appropriate—*becoming*.

Dying is a role we play like any other role in life: this is a troubling thought. You are never your true self except when you're alone—but who wants to be alone, dying?

But is it too much to want somebody somewhere to say something original about it?

Not long after her diagnosis, my friend attended a few sessions of group therapy. Although the sessions took place at the cancer clinic, the group was for patients only, without any professional therapist or other trained person to lead them. She wasn't surprised, my friend said, when everyone ended up saying the same things. Illness is a common experience, after all. Why wouldn't people respond to it in like ways?

There was one woman, my friend said, who joined the group around the same time that she did. This woman was around sixty, she'd been born in Bulgaria, and though she had lived in America since she was in high school she spoke English with an accent. She and her husband, of Bulgarian parents but American born, had been married for forty years. Retired now, her husband had worked all his life as a buildings inspector. She was a dental assistant. Three kids, all now grown. It had started out as a loving marriage, the woman told the group. She spoke of sweet memories of their early years: the wedding, the children's births in quick succession—all healthy and beautiful—granted like wishes, one two three.

But husband and wife had fallen out of love long ago, she said, and for most of the marriage they had not got along. In fact, the woman confessed, home was such a battleground that her children were glad when they were old enough to move out. After that, the couple fought less but led increasingly separate lives, she said. They slept in separate rooms, they did not always sit down to meals together. Whole days passed in which they exchanged barely a word. Still, they had taken a vow: for better, for worse. Plus, they were Catholic. There would be no divorce.

It had taken a while, the woman told the group, before they knew how sick she was. At first no one said anything about cancer. Her symptoms were probably caused by an ulcer, they said, or acid reflux, maybe even just a pulled muscle. The truth came in spurts, with one test after another bringing darker news than the last. (Grave nods from the group: this was a well-trod path.) Her husband's first response had been mostly irritation, the woman said. His wife had always been a hypochondriac, he told the doctor (not entirely without reason, his wife was willing to admit). He suffered from acid reflux himself, so what? Aches and pains—they were no spring chickens, either of them. But when a clear diagnosis of cancer was confirmed, the woman told the group, her husband changed.

At first, she said, she thought she might have been imagining it. Her children insisted that this was so—and no surprise, they said, given what she was going through. The shock. The fear. Not to mention the well-known disturbances of chemo brain.

But it was not her imagination, she said. Not shock, not fear, not chemo brain. Once the prognosis for metastatic pancreatic cancer had been explained to them, she said, her husband brightened up.

Suddenly he was always in a good mood around her, she said. Oh not that he enjoyed seeing her suffer, she said. He wasn't a monster. He was not the best of husbands, no, but he had always been a decent man. But he could not hide his feelings, she said. Not from her. In the hospital, she said, I would look at the other people visiting patients on my ward. I looked at their faces, and I looked at the faces of my children and my other family and friends, and I saw the same sadness and fear. But never a look like that from him, she said. And never tears. Once when he thought I was asleep I was actually secretly watching him, she told the group. He was sitting in a chair by the window, his legs crossed, swinging one foot. He was staring out the window with his face turned up toward the sky, and the look on his face was the look of a man contented, a man quite satisfied with the way things were. Then he stretched out his legs and leaned back with his hands clasped behind his neck, she said. Now he was studying the ceiling. After a few moments, as the woman described it, he breathed a deep sigh and broke into a smile.

According to my friend, the woman told the group that she had wanted to tell her husband to stay away, she did not want him to come to the hospital anymore. She wanted to tell him that he wasn't fooling her, she who knew him better than anyone—as if after forty years she could not tell what he was feeling. As if I could not read him like a book, she said. As if I could not hear his heart singing *Freedom*.

But she couldn't do it, she said. She did not have the courage to confront him, my friend told me the woman told the others in the group. The truth was, she felt bad for him. I was so ashamed of him, she said, that I pitied him. Though I hated him for not at least trying to hide his feelings, I thought maybe the truth was that he wasn't able to. I thought it was possible that he didn't even know this about himself, that he was in denial about his feelings (which would have been just like him, she said), and he would have been outraged if I—

And here she paused, needing a moment to collect herself.

Thinking about our life together, the woman resumed, what a misery our marriage had turned out to be, how little happiness we had to look back on, I had to confess that I understood. Perhaps, had their roles been reversed, she would have felt the same, she said. Perhaps many people trapped in bad marriages felt relief when the other one died. Perhaps they couldn't help feeling that way—and perhaps they couldn't hide their feelings. And terrible though all that was, the woman said she asked herself: Was it a crime? When you think about it, she said, what was I saying? That my husband should have been a better actor? A better liar?

She needed him, the woman went on. She was sick, she was flat on her back so many days, helpless. She didn't want to be a burden to her children, she said, each of whom had jobs and families and plenty of struggles of their own. She needed someone to take care of her, and her husband did take care of her, though God knows it wasn't always easy, and he did it without complaining.

And, as I say, the woman told the group, he is always in a good mood now. Always cheerful, only too happy to be doing this and that for me, sometimes humming under his breath, or whistling. And all along he has no idea what I'm going through, and that I know the truth. He has no idea, repeated the woman, that I know. I know.

According to my friend, the woman told her story in an oddly stilted and monotonous manner, keeping her eyes downcast, as if reading from an invisible script, auditioning for a part she had no hope of ever getting. But she had everyone's full attention, my friend said. You could've heard a pin drop, and of course we were all aghast at what we were hearing. When the woman finished, the others started talking. Not everyone, my friend said. There were some, like me, who didn't say anything (I confess I hadn't the faintest idea what to say to this poor woman), but the ones who did speak were in agreement. The woman was mistaken. Surely the children—who knew their own father, after all—were right, and the woman, who in their opinion must be completely wrong, should listen to them. There was another explanation for her husband's behavior, a perfectly obvious one, which was that it was just his way of coping, they said. And didn't it happen all the time. Isn't that what people did, they put on a bright face, they tried to act normal, to act cheerful, they hid their tears—and why? Because they thought this would make it easier for the patient and help her keep up her own spirits, that's why. And that's what her husband was doing, the people in the group explained to her. Nothing sinister about it. And hadn't she said herself how well he'd been taking care of her, that he was always there for her, that he couldn't do enough for her, and if that wasn't solid proof of his love—

The woman didn't argue with these people, reported my friend. In fact, she made no response to their comments, except to nod now and then, her eyes still always downcast, a crooked half-smile fixed on her face. *She knew.*

Now, here was this woman who'd gone and done the difficult thing, my friend said to me. She had looked at the truth, and she had not flinched. She had spoken the unspeakable. She had named names. And here were all these people, gaslighting her. They weren't being honest—not with her, not with themselves. Because they could not accept the truth, they had to bury it under a load of BS.

And it wasn't the first time something like that had happened in that room, my friend said. Always the same inane advice, the same clichés about the power of positive thinking and miracles happening and not giving up and letting cancer win. And all it did was remind her how hard it was for people to accept reality, my friend said to me. Our overpowering

need either to stick our heads in the sand or to sentimental-
ize everything, she said.

All of which reminded *me* how irritated my friend used
to get when other people insisted that, although her daughter
never showed her love, it had to be there. (*All children love
their mothers*: everyone knows that.)

Group therapy made her feel the opposite of supported,
my friend said. It made her feel alien. After the meeting at
which this woman had told her story, my friend said she'd
had enough. She never went back.

And later, when I heard that this woman had died, I felt
all that anger surging up again, she said. It seemed so terribly
wrong, the way her feelings had been denied, how none of us
had come up with a single thing to say that might have been
of any real help or comfort to her. Sick with shame was how
my friend described what she felt whenever she thought of
this woman now. And I kept wondering, she said, if there
ever came a time before the end when someone actually *saw*
this woman. Saw *her*.

This is the saddest story I have ever heard.

About this woman I myself am wondering: Did there
ever come a time before the end when she changed her mind
and confronted her husband after all?

What do you think is the meaning of your life?

"Family."

"Love."

"Doing the right thing."

"Being a good person."

"Staying positive and following your dream."

The meaning of life is that it stops. Of course it would have been a writer who came up with the answer. Of course that writer would have been Kafka.

But in your *own* words, the social worker says.

Those are my words. I'm agreeing with Kafka.

But the question is what is the meaning of *your* life.

That it stops, my friend says. Just like Kafka said. (Brittle little laugh.)

My wife and I have lived a long time, the owner of the house told me. And believe me, we're no strangers to tragedy. One of our children died of meningitis when she was just a tiny thing. At our age we've seen many of our friends and relatives pass, and, between the two of us, we've been through a few serious illnesses ourselves. A flooded house is not the worst thing in the world that can happen. If it's the worst thing that happens this year, I'll count myself lucky. That's the risk you take when you rent out your home, and of course that's why we have insurance. And it's a blessing that it wasn't the upstairs bath, in which case the damage would've been much worse.

We were on the phone. Before we hung up, something prompted me to ask him about the painting in the living room. (Watching over us—ha! said my friend, giving her the finger as we were vacating the house.) He told me that they'd bought it at an estate auction. We were both quite taken with it, he said. At first we thought it was a mistake, the way it dominated the living room. Then it turned out to be a good conversation piece. But my wife—no, she never looked anything like that, the man said. And he chuckled a bit.

Is that *you?* the water damage inspector asked me when he saw the painting.

11

If I'd kept a journal, I could tell you exactly when it was that we stopped speaking. By then, we were ensconced in my friend's apartment. After the house, the apartment felt small, but, again, I had my own room. I unpacked and settled in—again not knowing *for how long*—and took up the same routine. I did the grocery shopping and whatever other errands needed doing. The weekly housecleaner had been let go when my friend left the apartment for what she'd thought was for good, and so that job now also fell to me. I threw myself into it until she begged me to stop. The noise of the vacuum cleaner, the odor of disinfectant—these and other such ordinary stimuli had become intolerable to her. Her skin was now so sensitive that even silk could rub it raw.

But when she discovered her bedroom window fouled

with pigeon splat she insisted that I wash it right away. That done, we decided I should wash all the windows, much as the ammonia smell revolted her.

She was glad to be home, my friend said. She held on to the idea that going away had been a mistake, a surrender to faulty thinking, for which she'd been punished.

Now that she was back home, she would never leave the apartment again. Even when she was feeling well enough, she did not want to go out—not even to the park just across the street from her building, which had long been a favorite place of hers and was now, in midsummer, a haven of deep green shade. She had started having trouble with her balance and was terrified of falling. And there was something else: having reached the next—the final—stage of her journey, she had turned in on herself.

Returning from some errand, I sometimes stole a few minutes in the park before going indoors.

Usually, as soon as I sat down on one of the benches, I would cry.

Jesus, you know, it wasn't supposed to happen like this. Even if it strikes me now as having been inevitable. But doesn't love always feel just so: destined, no matter how unexpected, no matter how improbable.

Coincidence: in a new book I've been reading, I find someone comparing the experience of watching a person die with the intensity of falling in love. And you know, I wouldn't be surprised to learn that in some other language there's a word for this—like the word for that particular kind of love that in the language spoken by the Bodo people is called *onsra*.

I want to know what it will be like once all this (*all this*: the inexorable, the inexpressible) has become distant memory. I've always hated the way the most powerful experiences so often end up resembling dreams. I am talking about that taint of the surreal that besmears so much of our vision of the past. Why should so much that has happened feel as though it had not truly happened? *Life is but a dream.* Think: Could there be a *crueler* notion?

Memory. We need another word to describe the way we see past events that are still alive in us, thought Graham Greene.

Agreed.

Agreeing here also with Kafka. And, at the same time, with Camus: The literal meaning of life is whatever you do that stops you from killing yourself.

Whatever doesn't kill me makes me stronger. Dying, Christopher Hitchens asked himself how this bit of Nietzsche could ever have struck him as deep. Clearly it wasn't true to his own experience—and it hadn't been true to Nietzsche's, either. It was having cancer that had brought about this rethinking, Hitchens said.

How could I not now also recall the old graffiti "God is dead—Nietzsche, Nietzsche is dead—God." Later, anti-atheists could not resist replacing "Nietzsche" with "Hitchens."

Recent obits. I. M. Pei. Agnès Varda. Ricky Jay. Bibi Andersson. Doris Day.

Though not in that order (I liked the rhyme).

I've heard of people who confess to regularly reading obituaries in the hope of seeing the name of someone they know. Reading obituaries is also said to be a source of comfort to many lonely people. Presumably it's not the deaths that these people like reading about but the neatly summarized lives that the deceased supposedly lived. But are these same people also avid readers of biographies? Probably not. *Write your own obituary*: an exercise often recommended by life coaches and human-development counselors, and one that has never had the tiniest shred of appeal for me.

It is from death that the storyteller derives his authority, wrote Walter Benjamin, in his authoritative way. And: the "meaning of life" is the center about which the novel moves.

Bart Starr. Carol Channing. W. S. Merwin. Michel Legrand.

Who, coincidentally, wrote the score for *The Umbrellas of Cherbourg.*

Most of these people were long-lived, almost all having survived well past the average human life span of seventy-nine years. My friend, not young at all, was nevertheless young enough to have been their daughter.

John Paul Stevens. Toni Morrison. Paul Taylor. Hal Prince.

Chaser, "the world's smartest dog." Sarah, "the world's smartest chimp."

Grumpy Cat!

The last of his kind. On New Year's Day, 2019, in a university breeding facility in Hawaii, a fourteen-year-old tree snail named George died. And with that his entire species went extinct.

I didn't mean to say that we just stopped speaking, abruptly. It was not like that. Even before the disaster that forced us to vacate the house, we'd stopped having the kind of conversation that sometimes left my friend coughing or out of breath. It wasn't that we had nothing more to say to each other but rather that our need for speech kept diminishing. A look, a gesture or touch—sometimes not even that much—and all was understood.

The farther along she was on her journey, the less she wanted to be distracted.

She no longer wanted to be read to, though she was able again to do some reading herself. While we were gone a package had arrived: the galleys of a book, the author someone she knew, a former student, asking for a blurb.

One last good deed, my friend said. Why not.

It would be the last book she read. (I'd like to say, for effect, that the blurb was the last thing she wrote but, although that's perfectly possible, I don't know for sure if it's correct.)

Let me not forget our last good laugh together.

We had loaded the car with our things and were driving

away from the house. We had gone a few miles in silence when she blurted in a small, woeful voice: You work, you plan.

Could I have heard her right? Those words were a piece of dialogue from one of the movies we'd watched together, an old screwball comedy in which a playboy courts an heiress, plotting to enrich himself by first marrying and subsequently doing away with her. *Damn, damn, damn*, the cad cries in exasperation when all goes amiss. *You work, you plan, nothing ever turns out the way it's supposed to!* This scene had had us in stitches, and now, in spite of the fact that she was obviously upset, her words struck me as so outrageous under the circumstances that all I could do was laugh. Startled at first, she joined in.

After we'd calmed down and driven another few miles, I said that I hoped this time she hadn't left the pills behind. Which set us off again. *Lucy and Ethel Do Euthanasia.* I was shaking so hard that the car veered a little off the road.

No, she didn't want any visitors. She had said her goodbyes, she said.

No, she did not want to reach out one last time to her daughter.

I am reconciled to our not being reconciled, she said.

Once, sitting in the park across the street, I scanned the front of her building. Which windows were hers? I counted the floors—and there she was! Standing at a sixth-floor window—her bedroom window—looking out. From there she would have had a good view of the park. But did she see me? From what I could tell she wasn't looking down at the street but into the distance. I thought of waving, but it was too late: she was gone. (Even so, as often happens, imagination would become memory: I would recall the sight of my friend waving to me from that bedroom window again and again.) It was this glimpse of her, though, that made me think of another woman, someone I had known briefly many years ago.

I was in between college and grad school then, a time in my life when I made ends meet by stringing together various part-time jobs, and this woman had hired me to do some research for a book she was writing. She too lived in an apartment with a view of a park: a much grander apartment, a much larger park. Central Park. She was about twenty years older than me, and the book she was writing was a biography of a woman from an old rich American family who'd found fame as a model and actress in the 1960s but whose psychological disorders had led to self-destructive misery and untimely death.

Aside from the book, which was apparently giving her enormous trouble, the woman was pursuing other projects. She had me call several literary agents to ask for copies of manuscripts by writers whom they represented. (I don't remember exactly what this was about, most likely she was looking for something to develop as a film.) The agents all seemed to know who she was but did not seem to take her seriously, and a few let me know that they were busy people who didn't appreciate being bothered in this way. When I reported that one of them had said something highly insulting—something like "You girls should find yourselves another game to play"—instead of being highly insulted she was amused.

Once, she gave me a list of names and phone numbers of people she wanted me to call to invite to a party. Just about every name on the list was recognizable to me; several would have been recognizable to anyone.

I didn't like the job, because it never felt quite real to me; it *did* often seem like just a game. I didn't have much faith that this woman would ever finish the book she was writing. Also, the pay was low.

One morning she called me at home and asked me to go that same day to a certain archival library and ask for a certain book. She wanted me to go through this book, an antique bound typescript that was not permitted to be taken out, and cull from it specific details about the lives of the people of whom the woman she was writing about was a descendant. She said that I should call ahead and ask to have the book waiting for me when I arrived. But I didn't call ahead—I doubted that this was really necessary—and was surprised when I had to wait more than an hour for it to be brought to me.

When she saw my bill for that day's work, she questioned the amount. When I explained about the wait, she reminded me that she had told me to call ahead; if I had done so there wouldn't have been a wait, she said. We had words then. In the end she agreed to pay me for the extra hour and would have been happy to move on. But I didn't want to work for her after that, and I never did again.

All this was more than forty years ago. In all that time I rarely thought about her, though I was aware that she did in fact finish her book and that it had been published. From time to time, I'd hear something about one of her glamorous parties. But as one who does not regularly read obituaries, I missed hers when it first appeared, and it wasn't until just recently that I learned that, a few years ago, she had jumped from the penthouse apartment where she had moved sometime after I last saw her.

None of the photographs that were published with the obituaries I have seen showed her as she was at the time of death: old—about twice the age as when we first met—and depressed. Most matched the image in my head: curly dark hair, toothy smile in a thin bony face. She had a frothy ever-excited-sounding voice and a tendency to gush: Everyone was adorable. Everything was divine. The silver (or they might have been gold) ballet flats she wore around the house. Her jagged penmanship, like a drunk's or a child's. An exaggerated fear of getting sick. (Do you have a cold? I won't go near my own children when they have a cold.) Shuddering as she told me about a close friend who'd found what turned out to be a malignant tumor in her neck. And it was just this tiny lump, she wailed. Gingerly palpating her own long thin neck.

The gracious host. At our first meeting, when she was interviewing me for the job, a maid entered the room carrying a tray: white wine, crackers, and pâté, the pâté served in a small clay flowerpot. The gauche guest: after a too tightly held cracker snapped between my fingers I was too self-conscious to touch anything else.

From the obituaries and in memoriam pieces I learned several things about her that I hadn't known before and was reminded of other things that I had known once but had completely forgotten. It was often recalled that, while she was still in school, she had had an affair with old William Faulkner.

A moment of remembrance, then, as I sat in the park, looking up at my friend's windows. Those windows that had just been scrubbed as clean as Orwell's ideal prose.

At my side: my grocery bags, the eggs and bread and salmon and kale and ice cream that she will never eat. That I will eat and eat until I am so full that I can eat no more. Yet will eat more.

Along comes a man with a broom and a long-handled dustpan. I know him. He is a neighborhood volunteer who keeps the park free of litter, bless him.

And bless the woman who comes each day to feed the squirrels and the birds.

Bless the squirrels and the birds.

But now that couple, across from me. They have just sat down, a young couple, and they are arguing. I can't hear them well over the fountain's burble and splash, but I believe they are speaking French. They have sat down on the edge of the fountain. They are young and they are beautiful— even in anger, they are beautiful, the way young people are. I do not know what they are saying but I can tell—you can always tell—that they are fighting.

Oh, please don't fight, young people. Let this be a place of peace.

I too had a fight with someone, this very morning, I could tell them. I could interrupt the couple right now, like a crazy lady, the sort of crazy lady you meet in the park. Break into the middle of their fight, start telling them all about my own fight, the fight I had this morning on the phone with my ex. Because I told him I was afraid I couldn't do it, I did not think that I could lie. We were going over it all, once again. If you are present at the time of death, he said, it's a given that you'll be questioned. I know, I know, I said, because of course I did know—how many times had we been over this? But I could imagine how, in that very moment, it might be hard for me to lie. Or, at least, to lie convincingly.

Was all I said.

He blew up then. This is so like you, he said. Also for the umpteenth time. He said, You are impossible.

This is so like you. Everything that bothered him, every-thing that went wrong between us, was always *so like me.*

It was so like me not to have made him happy. So like me to have driven him away. To have forced him to seek comfort in somebody else's arms—that was so fucking like me.

He actually said.

Yelled, in fact.

Imagine the young couple exchanging bewildered looks. Why is she telling us all this?

Or why not imagine them kind. Forgetting their fight, putting aside their own troubles to listen. *Quel est ton tourment?*

A folie à deux was how my ex described what was happening between my friend and me.

He washed his hands of us.

Crazy lady. Talk about your biggest fear. Crazy old lady with her bags on a park bench. Blessing things, cursing things. That kind of woman's story. A fate my own mother barely escaped. I should get up and go now. The ice cream is melting. The fish will spoil. But my head is light. I'm afraid if I stand up I'll be dizzy. Panic strikes. What is happening here?

The man with his broom and dustpan, the feeder of squirrels and birds have both moved on. The French couple (oh good: they must have made up, he has his arm around her, her head is on his chest) are moving on.

What is happening? My heart throbs with fear. Soon it will end, this fairy tale. This saddest time that has also been one of the happiest times in my life will pass. And I'll be alone.

Blessed are they that mourn.

What draws the reader to the novel is the hope of warming his shivering life with a death he reads about, said Benjamin.

I have tried. I have put down one word after the other. Knowing that every word could have been different. As my friend's life, like any other life, could have been different.

I have tried.

Love and honor and pity and pride and compassion and sacrifice—

What does it matter if I failed.

ACKNOWLEDGMENTS

Special thanks to Joy Harris and to Sarah McGrath.

I am also deeply grateful to the Ucross Foundation, the Djerassi Resident Artists Program, the James Merrill House Writer-in-Residence Program, and the MacDowell Colony for their generous support.

CREDITS

Quote on page 1: Simone Weil, "Reflections on the Right
Use of School Studies with a View to the Love of God,"
Waiting for God, trans. Emma Craufurd
(New York: HarperCollins, 2009).
Quote on page 115: Jules Renard, *The Journal of Jules Renard,*
trans. and ed. Louise Bogan and Elizabeth Roget
(Portland, Ore., and Brooklyn, N.Y.: Tin House Books, 2008).
Quote on page 179: Inger Christensen, *The Condition of Secrecy,*
trans. Susanna Nied (New York: New Directions, 2018).